Snowflake and Sacred Movements

Dan Fallon

Illustrations by Paul Winward

Author – Daniel Fallon
Illustrator – Paul Winward
First published in 2016 by The Lifelong Workshops Ltd
Copyright © 2016 Daniel Fallon, The Lifelong Workshops Ltd
ISBN 978-1534656284

This is the first edition published 2016
© 2016 Daniel Fallon, The Lifelong Workshops Ltd

All rights reserved, permitted by the UK Copyright, Designs and Patents Act 1988

Registered Office
The Lifelong Workshops Ltd, Fallon House, 1st Floor
20 Stonebridge Avenue, Hull, HU9 5AY, United Kingdom

No part of this publication may be reproduced or distributed in any form or by any means, electronic or mechanical, or stored as a database retrieval system, without prior written permission from the publisher.

This book is for educational purposes. The publisher and author of this instructional book are not responsible in any manner whatsoever for any adverse effects arising directly or indirectly as a result of the information provided in this book. If not practised safely with caution, working out can be dangerous to you and others. It is important to consult with a professional fitness instructor (like Snowflake) before beginning training.

Chapter One

Snowflake's Adventures on Mount Lifelong

Snowflake was born in the Green Bingo Jungle. He was born with beautiful white hair and pale pink skin. He was the only one of his kind; unique in every way possible.

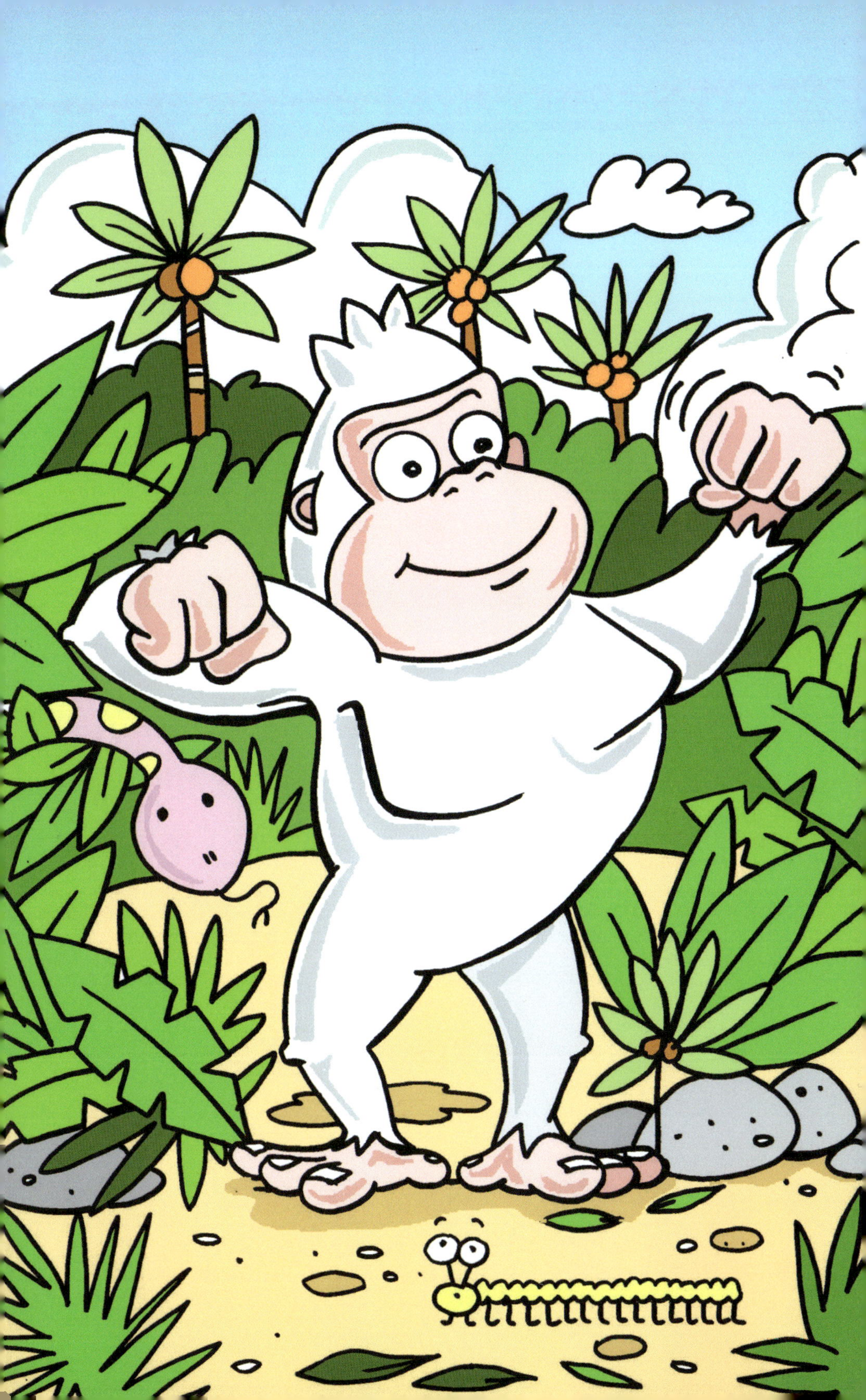

As he was growing up, Snowflake knew that he was born to make a difference in the world – to bring about a change. But what that change would be, he did not know.

One day when Snowflake was travelling through the Green Bingo Jungle he came across Charlie, a wise old silverback gorilla.

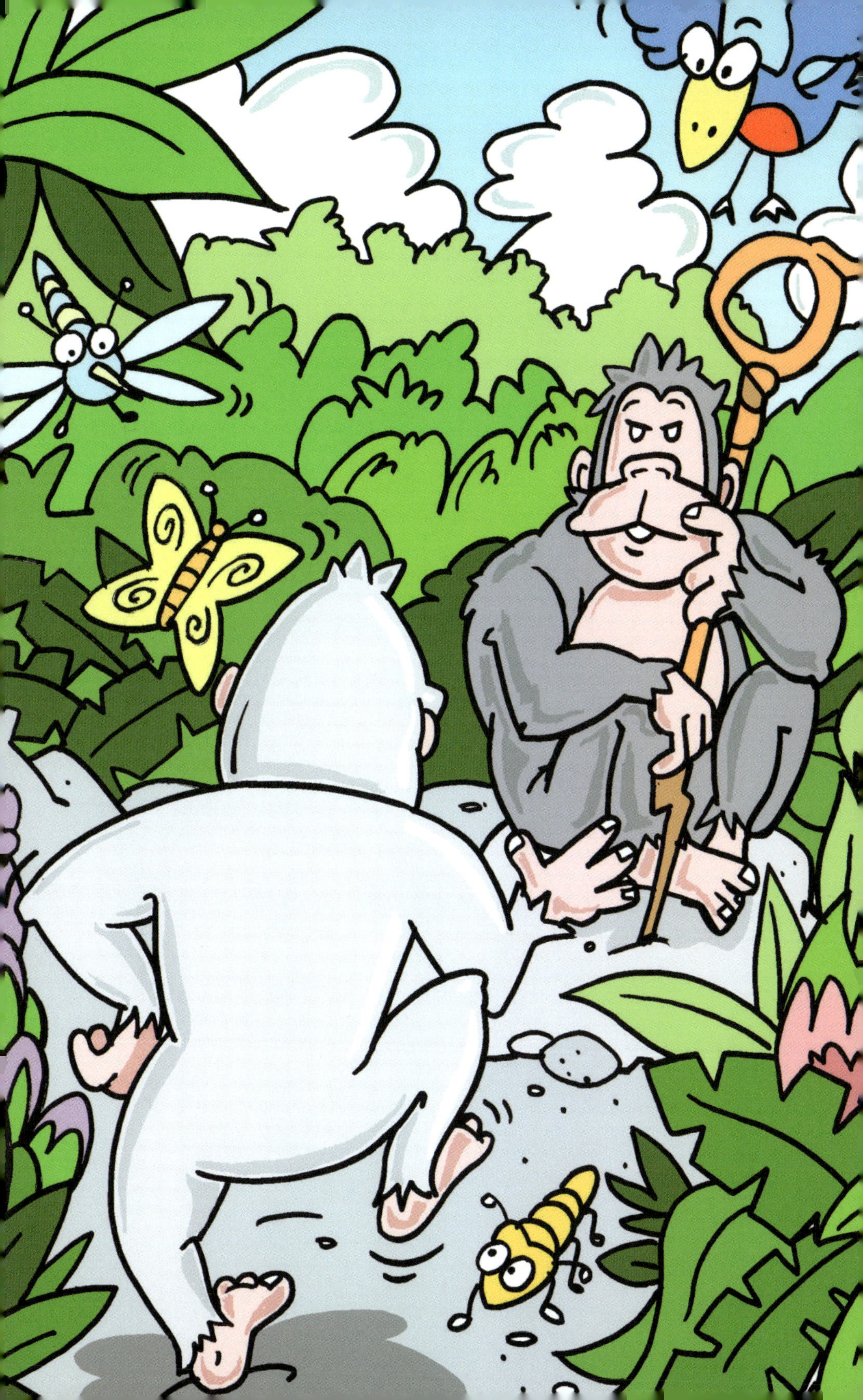

Charlie was amazed to see Snowflake. 'You are the One!' he screamed, dancing around with his old cane.

Snowflake was confused. He was the only white gorilla in the world, and always seemed to draw attention. 'I'm sorry,' he said to Charlie.

'Why are you sorry? You are the One!' Charlie said excitedly.

'I don't understand,' replied Snowflake. 'The One? Why am I the One?'

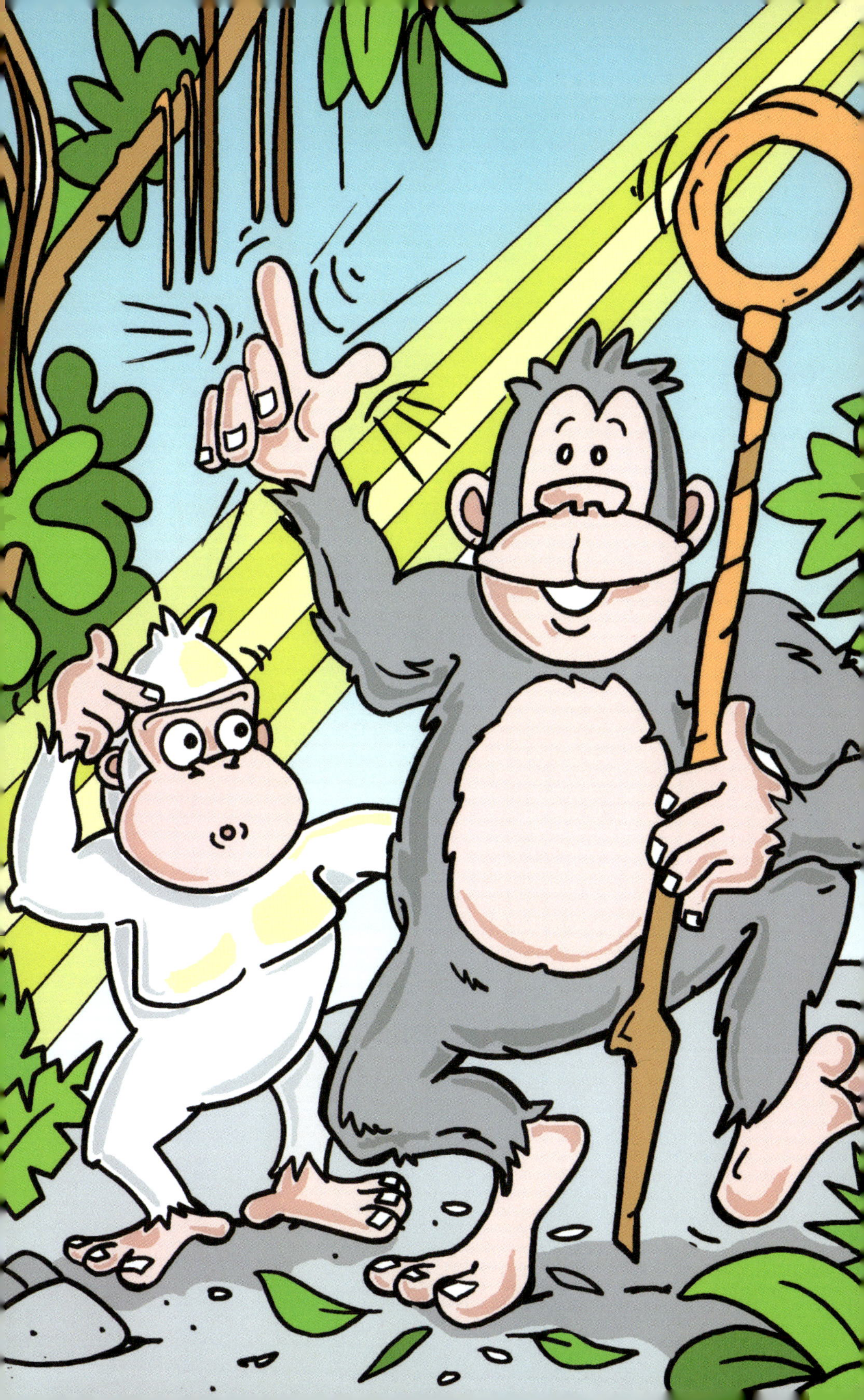

'My grandfather dreamed of the day that I would meet the White Gorilla and teach him the way to climb Mount Lifelong to discover the meaning of life,' Charlie explained.

'Wow!' Snowflake replied. He did not know what to say. For years, gorillas had tried to climb the famous mountain but had always failed. Now Charlie was telling Snowflake that he would succeed, and would change the world forever.

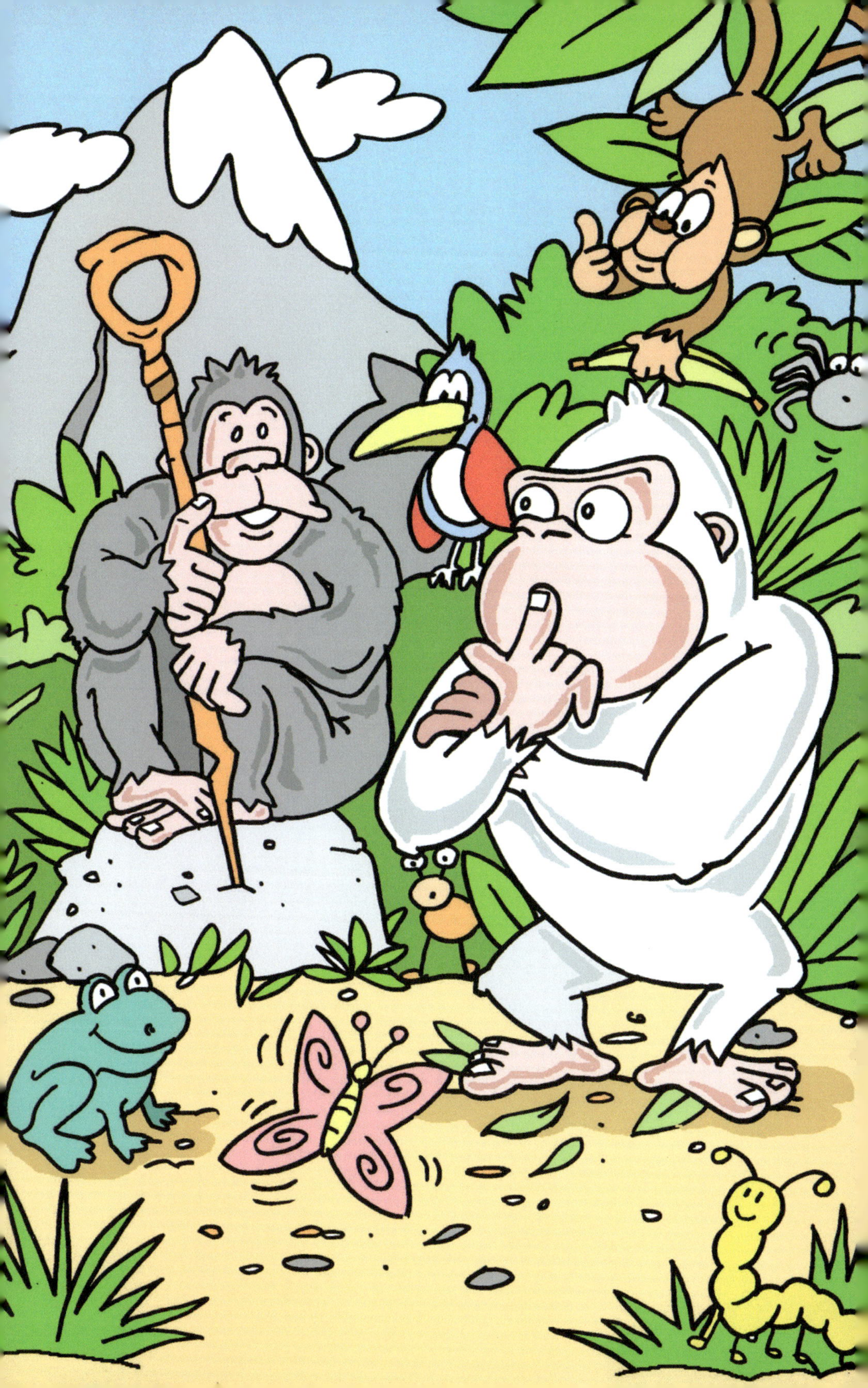

Snowflake had always wanted to climb Mount Lifelong and find the meaning of life, but never believed he could be successful. Until now!

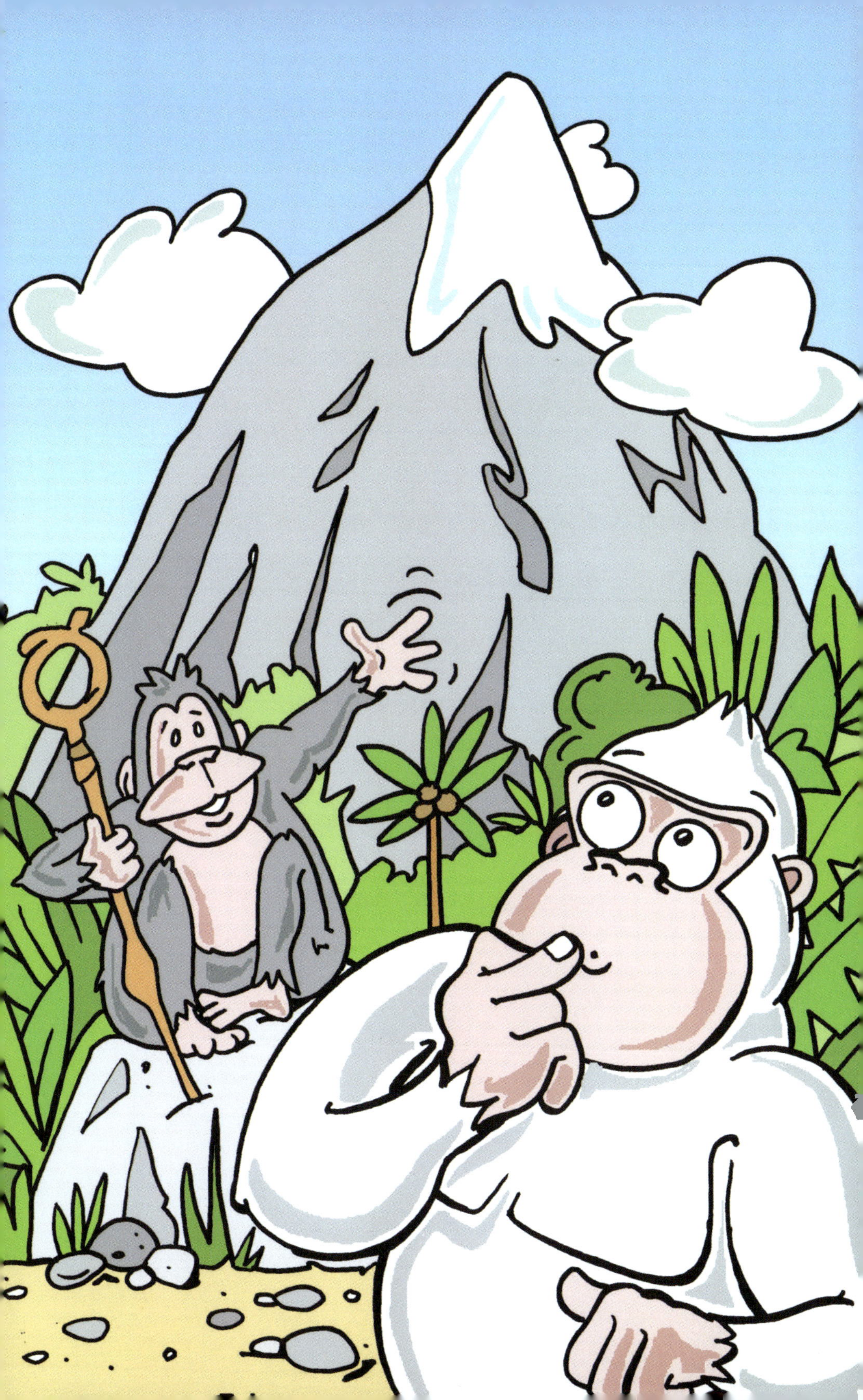

Charlie told Snowflake that before he made his journey, he must learn the Seven Sacred Movements. These movements had been passed down through Charlie's family for centuries, ready for the day that the White Gorilla was found in the Green Bingo Jungle.

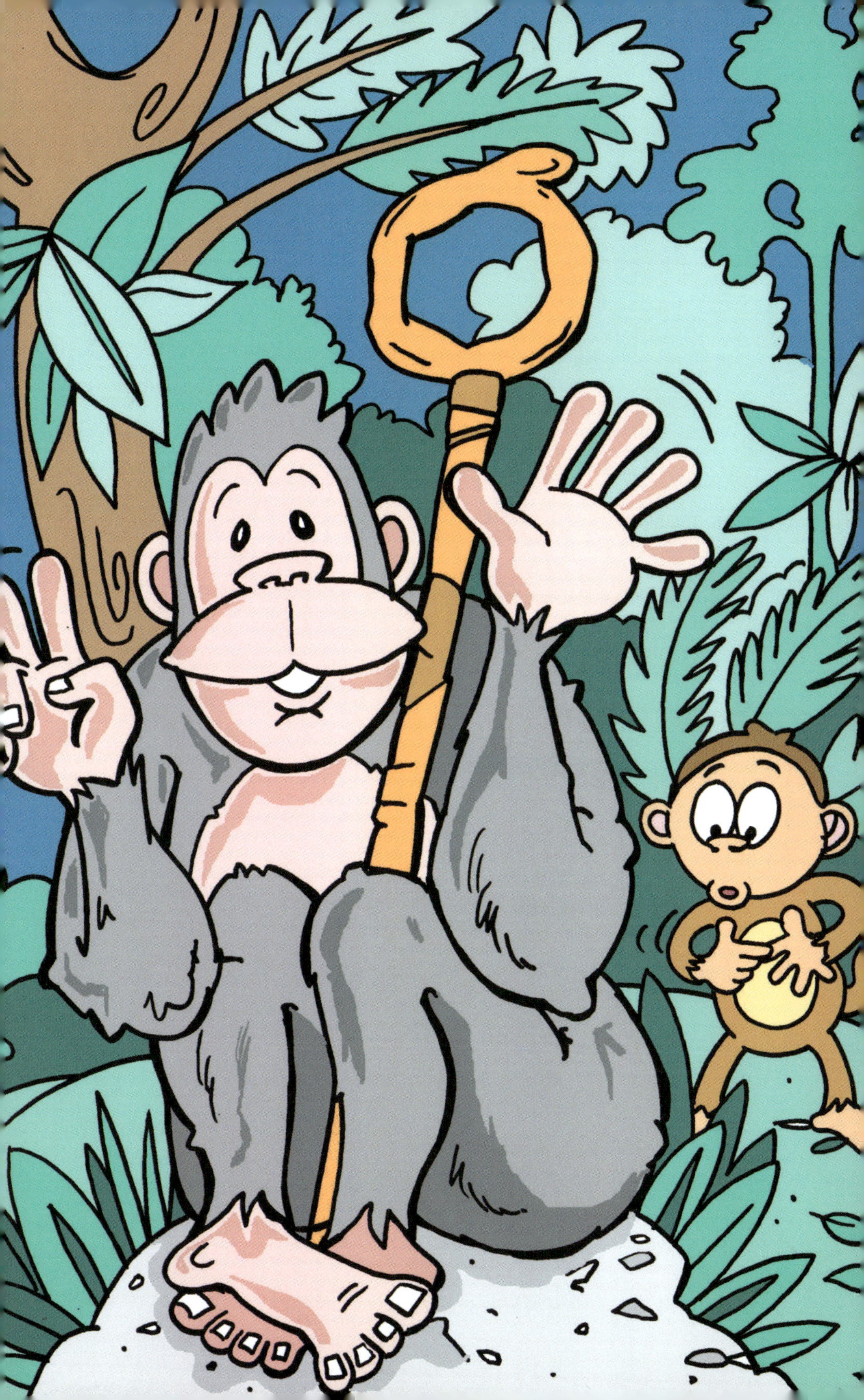

'Today, we will begin your training,' Charlie told Snowflake. 'The Seven Sacred Movements have magical powers, when they are performed from the heart with passion and commitment.' Charlie explained to Snowflake how the movements would keep him strong and allow him to stay as safe as possible. The adventure had begun!

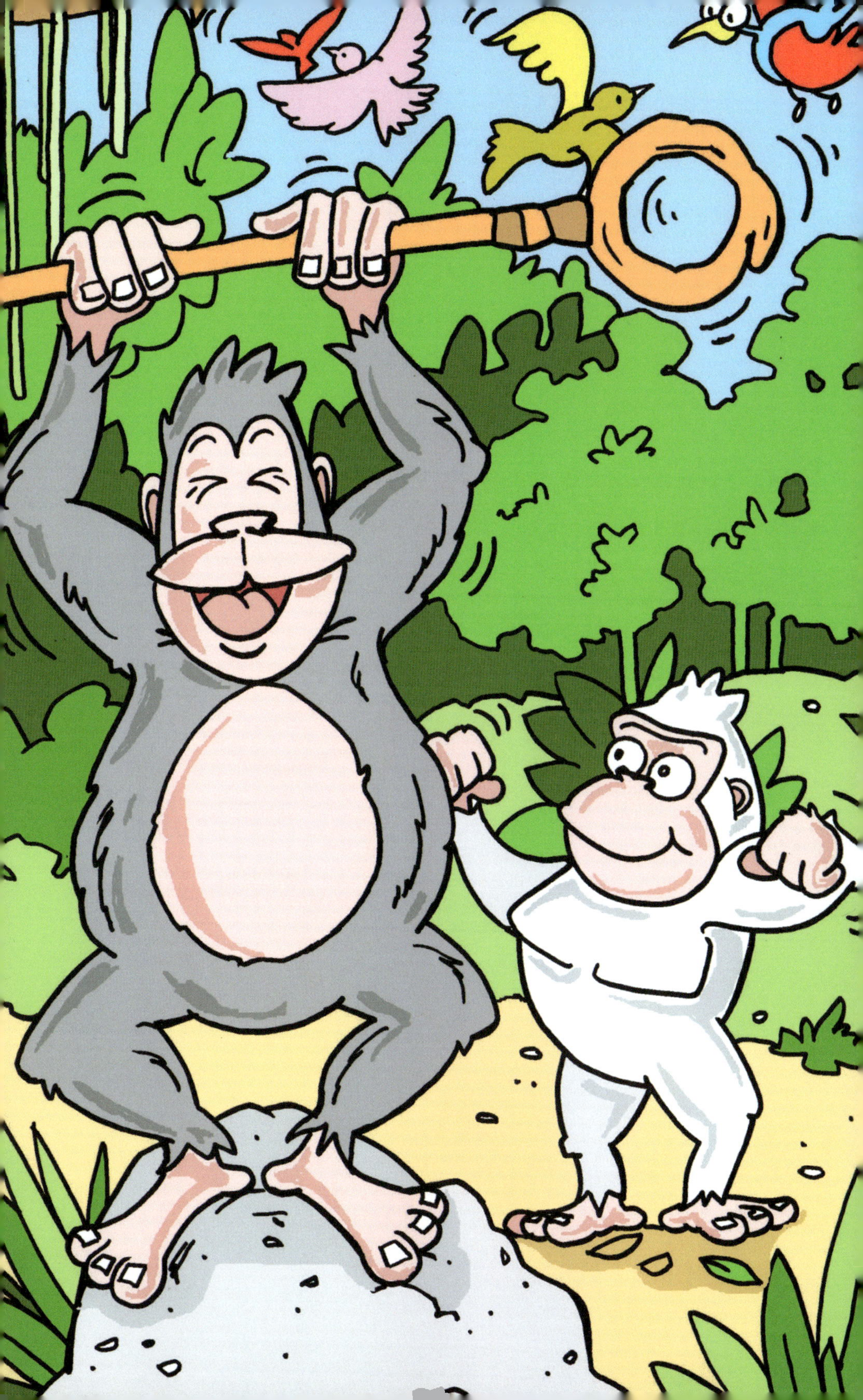

Snowflake begins to learn the Seven Sacred Movements

The **Silent Squat** brings silence and clarity to you when you are confused and need to see clearly. Just sit in the Silent Squat position and your vision will become clear.

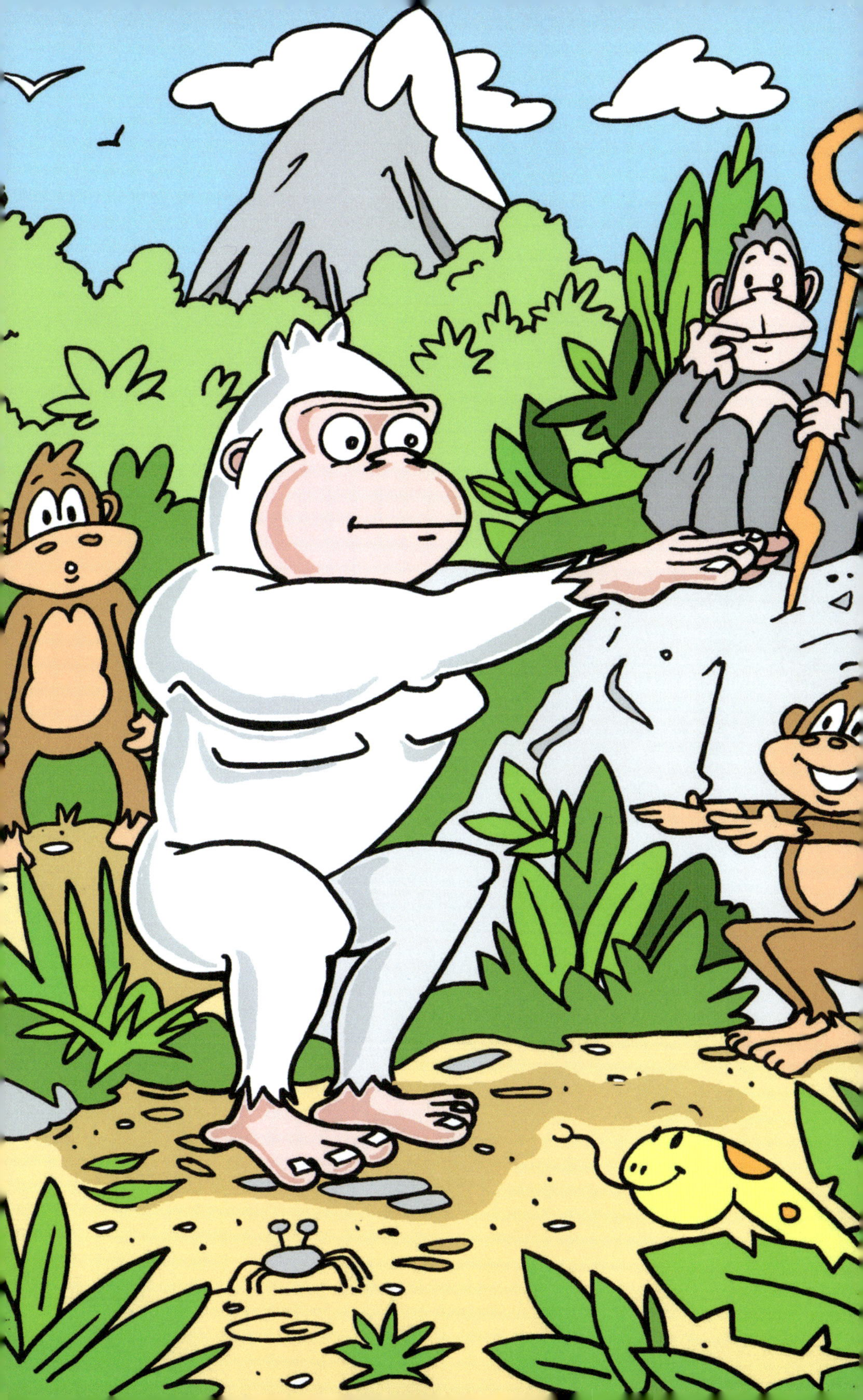

The **Limitless Lunge** can take you back in time to see if you have made the same mistake before. It is very important when facing danger to avoid repeating your earlier mistakes.

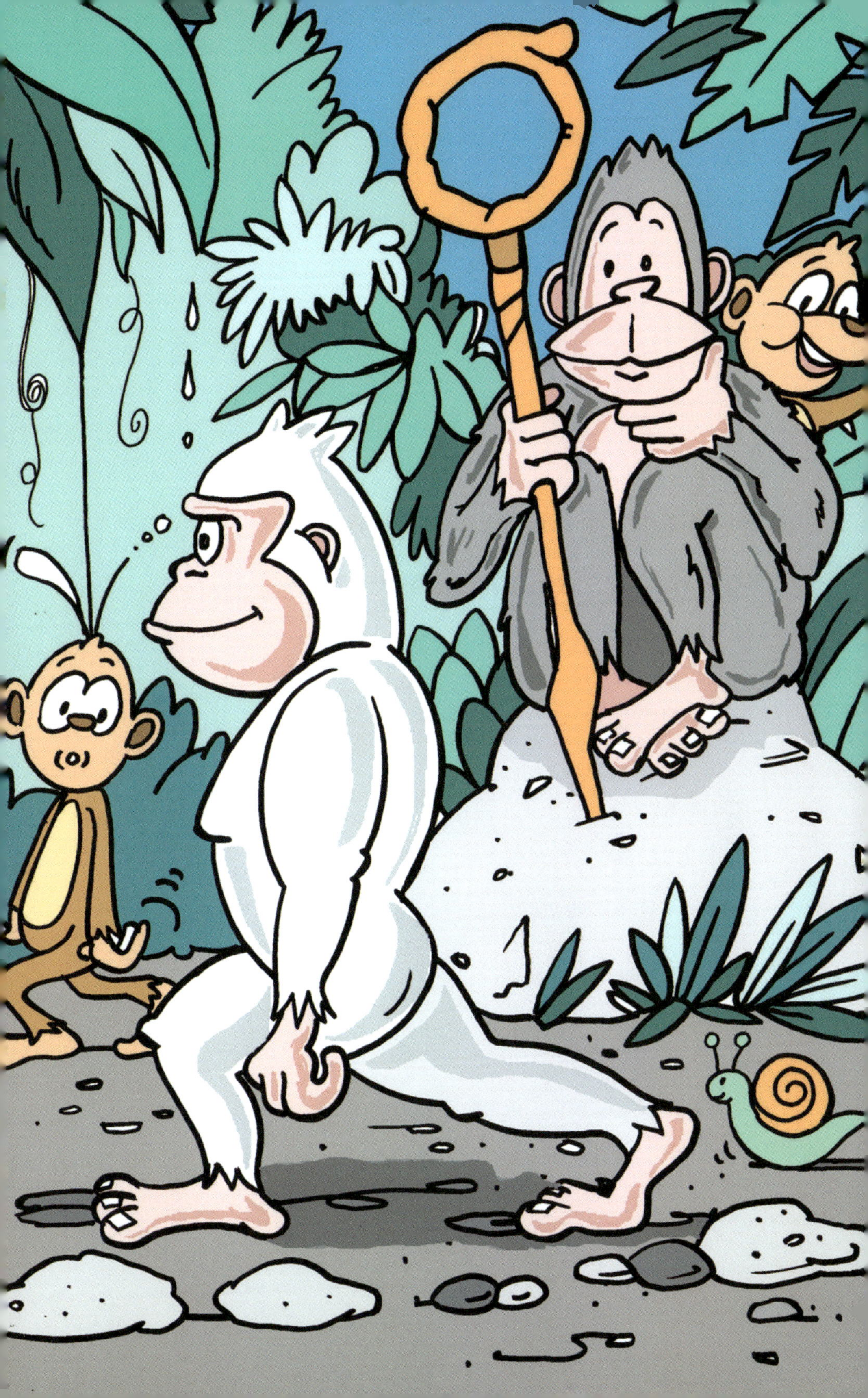

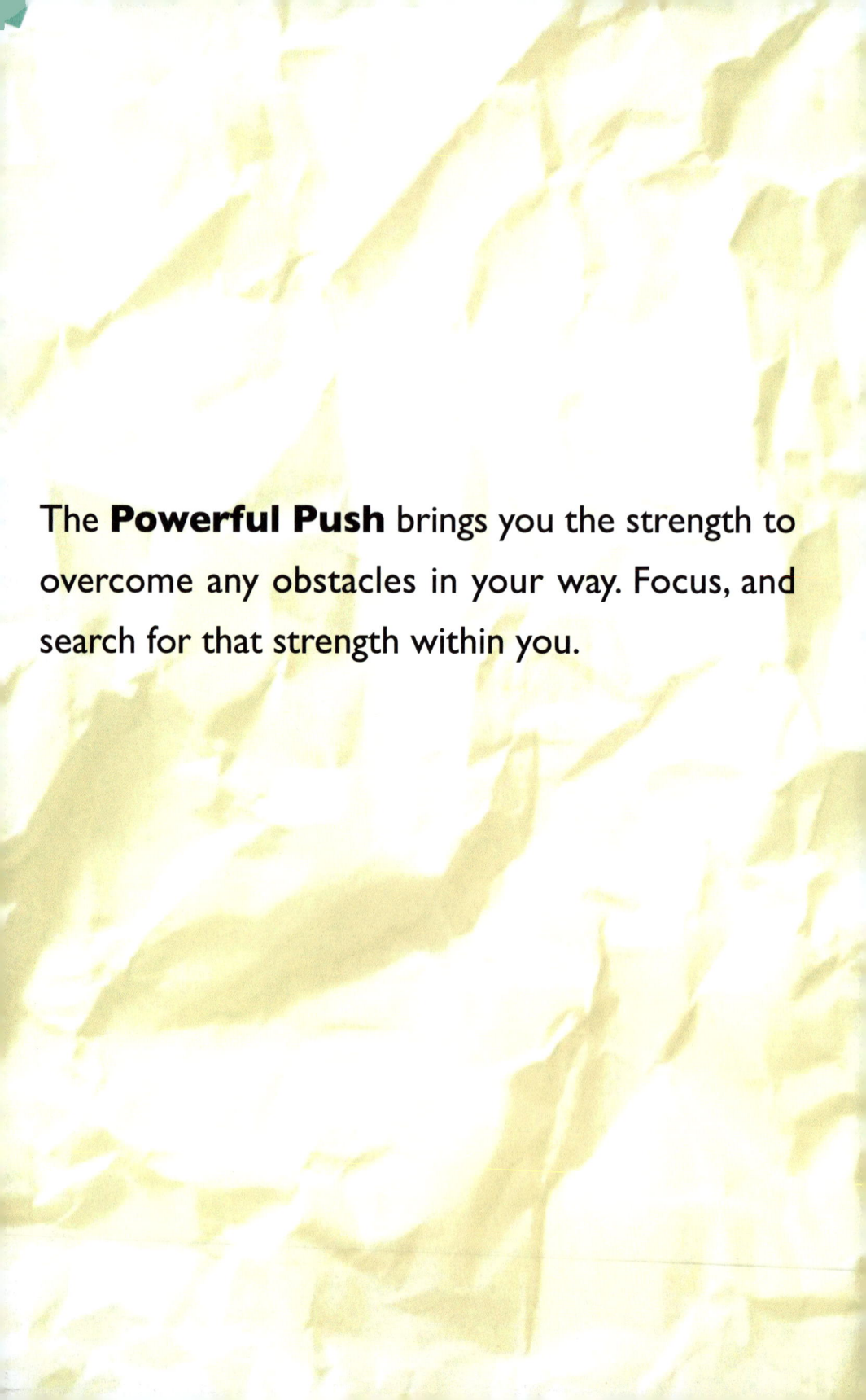

The **Powerful Push** brings you the strength to overcome any obstacles in your way. Focus, and search for that strength within you.

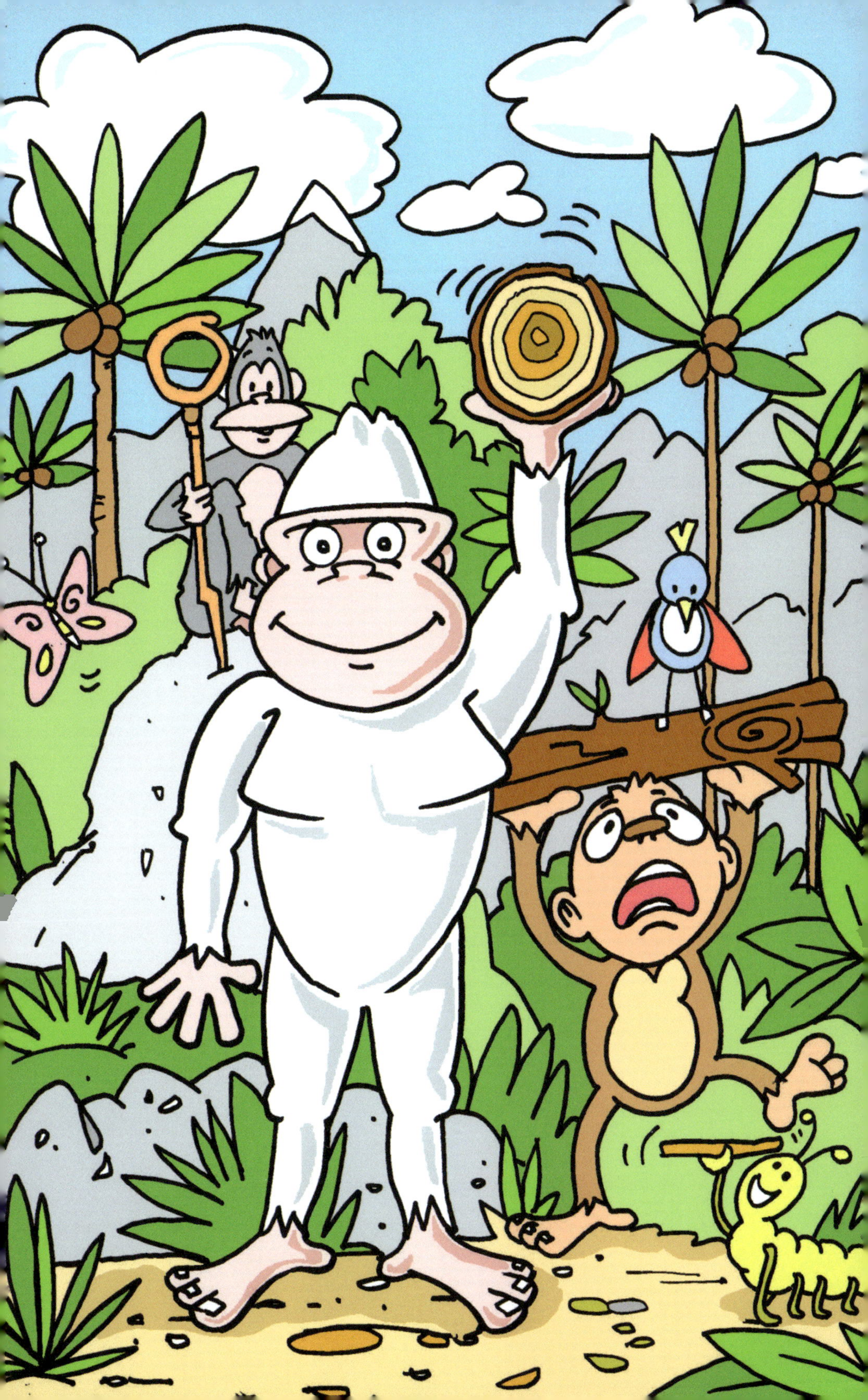

The **Peaceful Pull** allows you to restore your energy; to recharge yourself when you are running low. If we push, we must also pull – this is the balance.

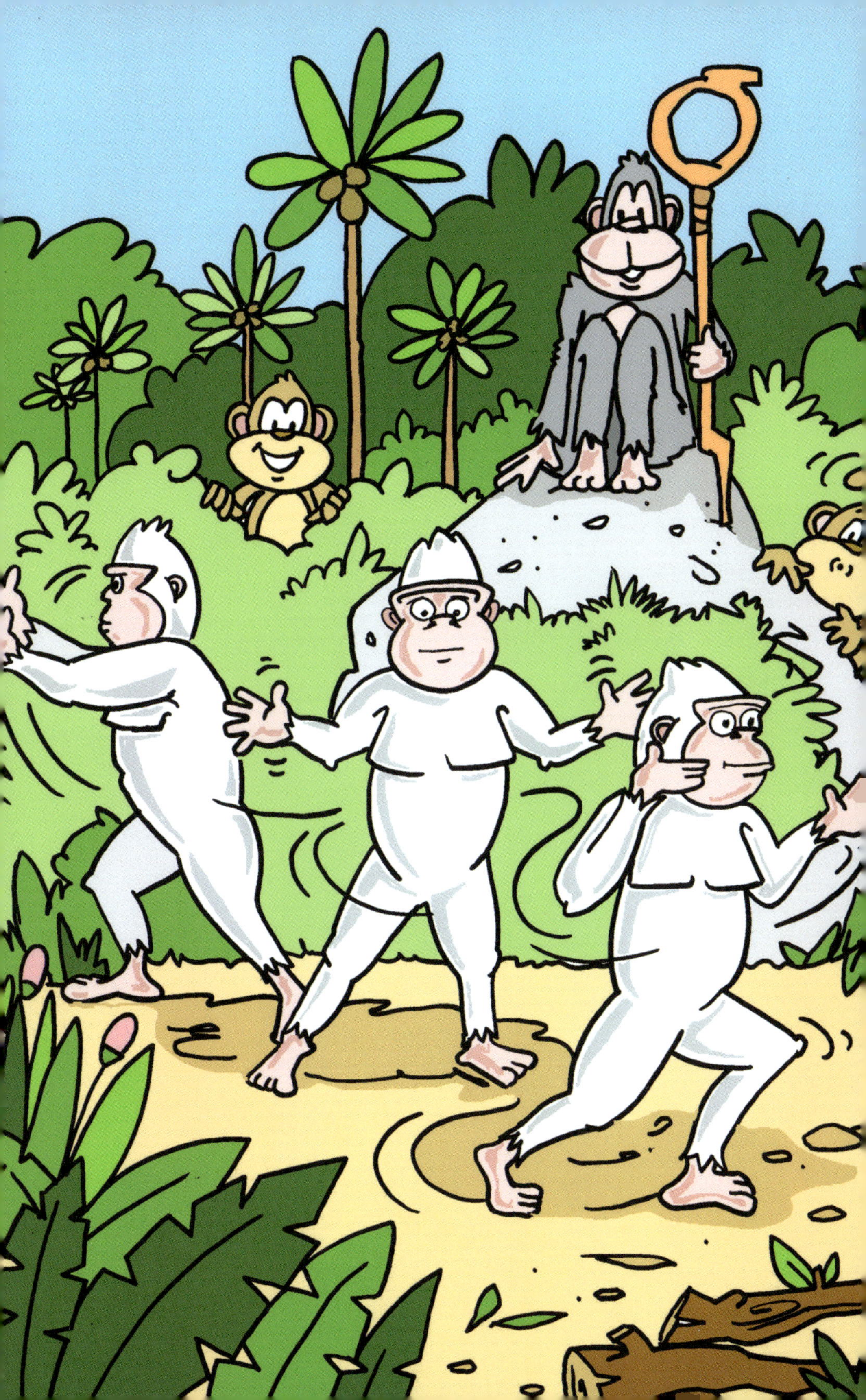

The **Brave Bend** brings you the courage to lift the heaviest of objects. The strength of ten gorillas lives within this movement.

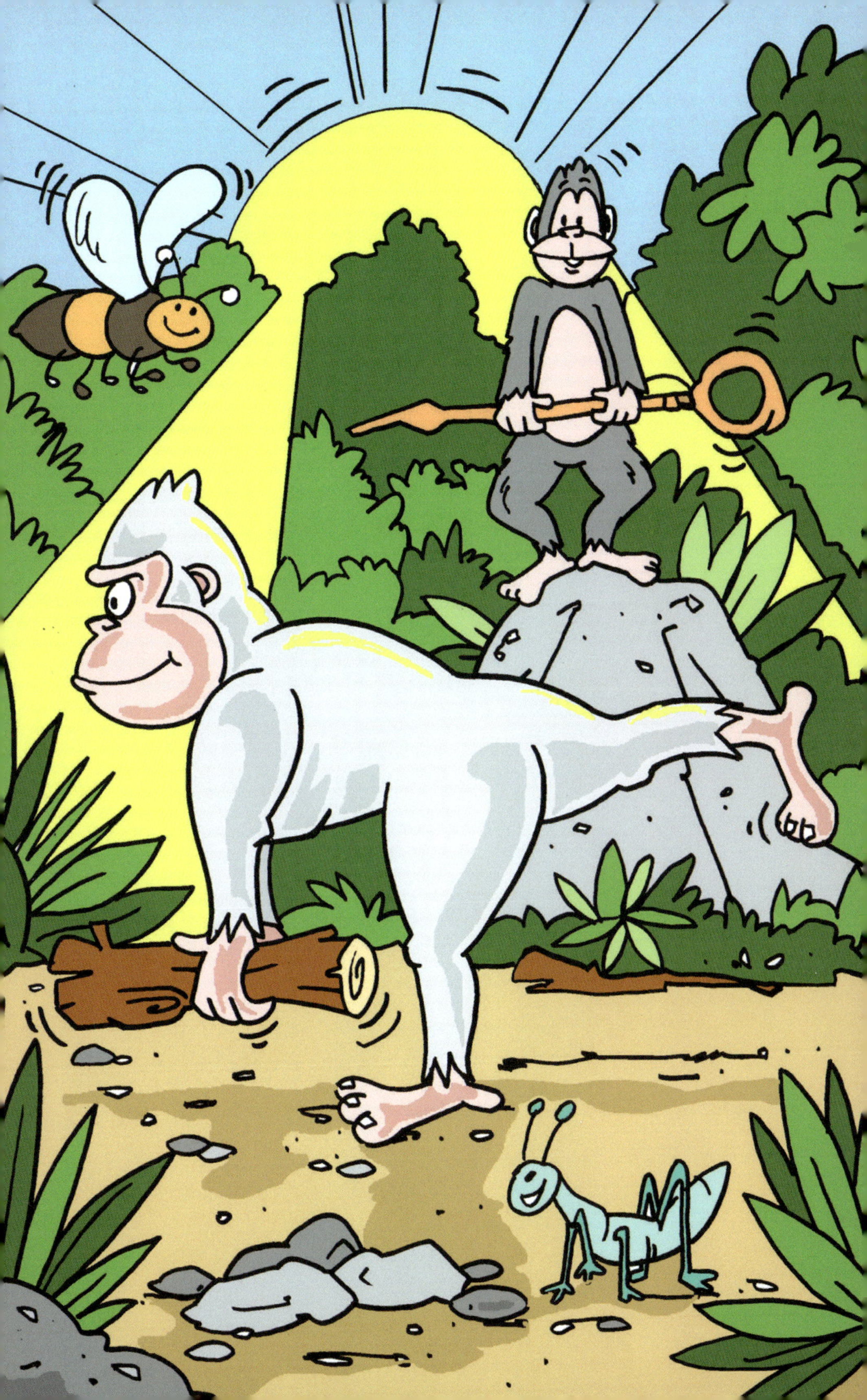

The **Tornado Twist** unlocks the elements (earth, wind, fire and water). Use this movement wisely, and stay safe.

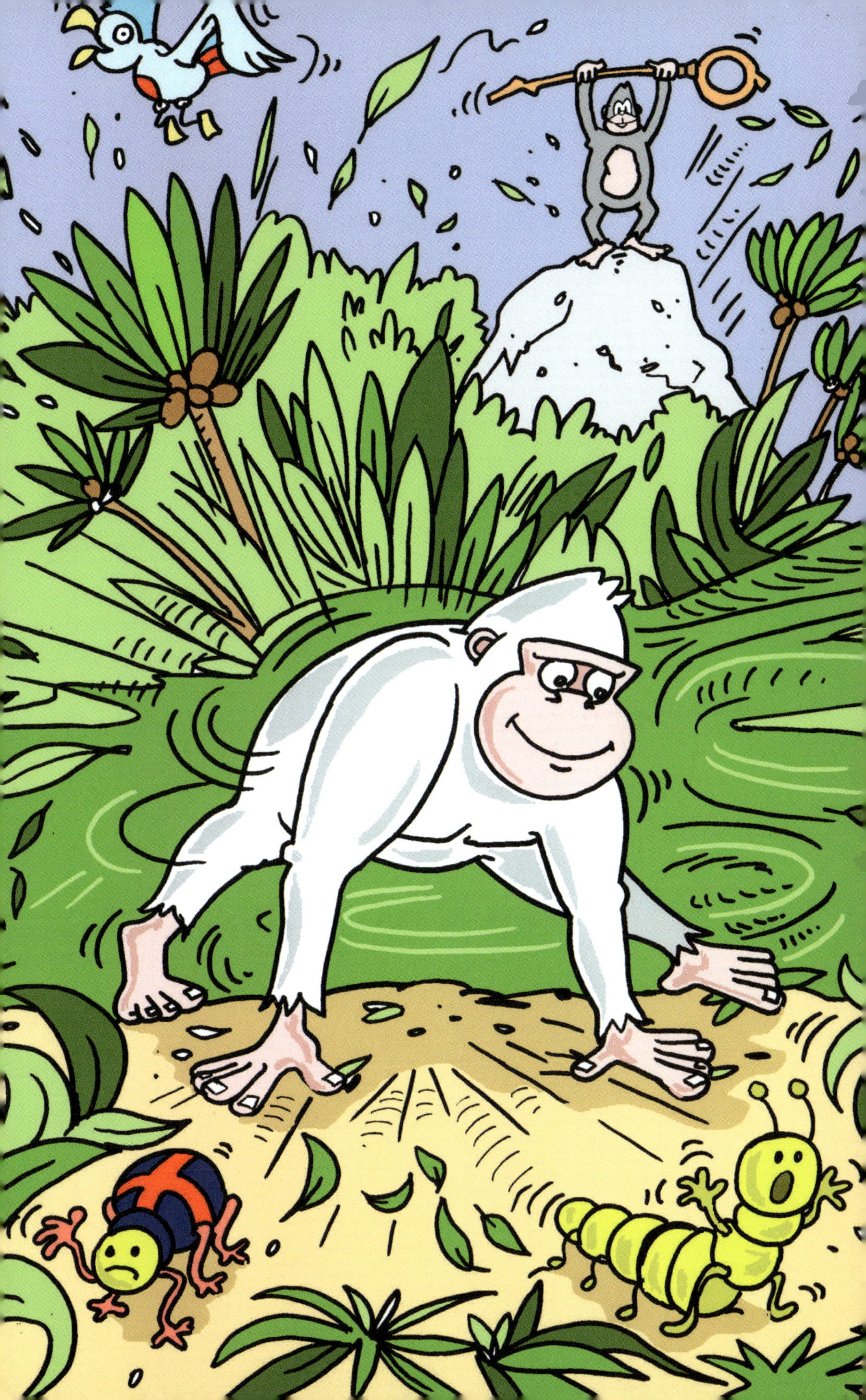

The **White Tiger Walk** is the last of the Seven Sacred Movements. These tigers have not been seen for fifty years, but legend tells us that when you walk as the White Tiger does, his wisdom becomes yours. You will then have the key to unlock the meaning of life at the top of Mount Lifelong.

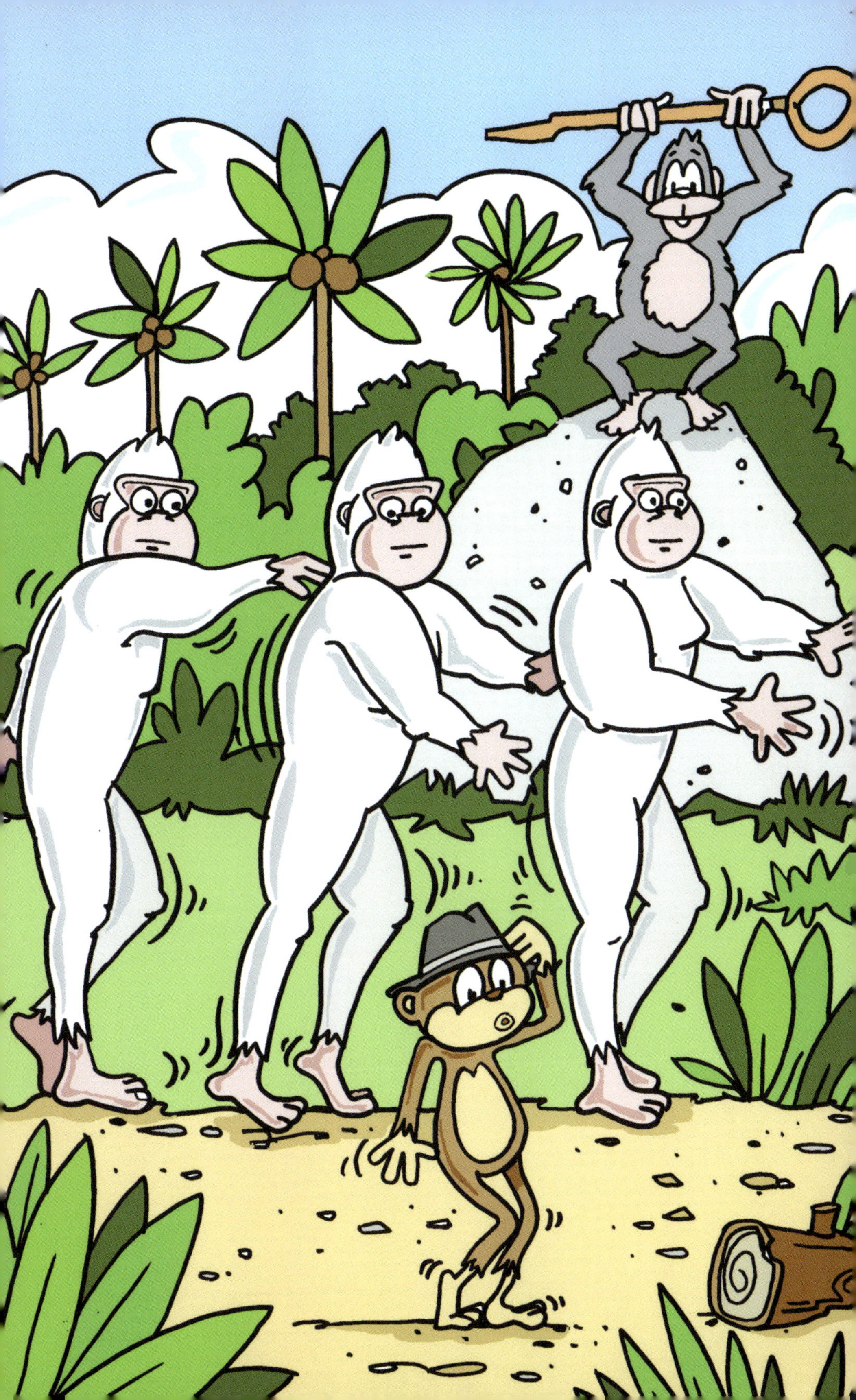

With Charlie's guidance, Snowflake worked hard to learn the Seven Sacred Movements. One day, he realised that he was ready to journey to the top of Mount Lifelong to find the meaning of life. He had learned that with passion and commitment, anything is possible.

Chapter Two

The Journey to River Rose

Boom! Crash! Boom!

Snowflake woke up with a start and jumped out of the tree where he had been sleeping all night. A great big cloud of dust was coming towards him. Soon, out of the dust, a herd of elephants appeared.

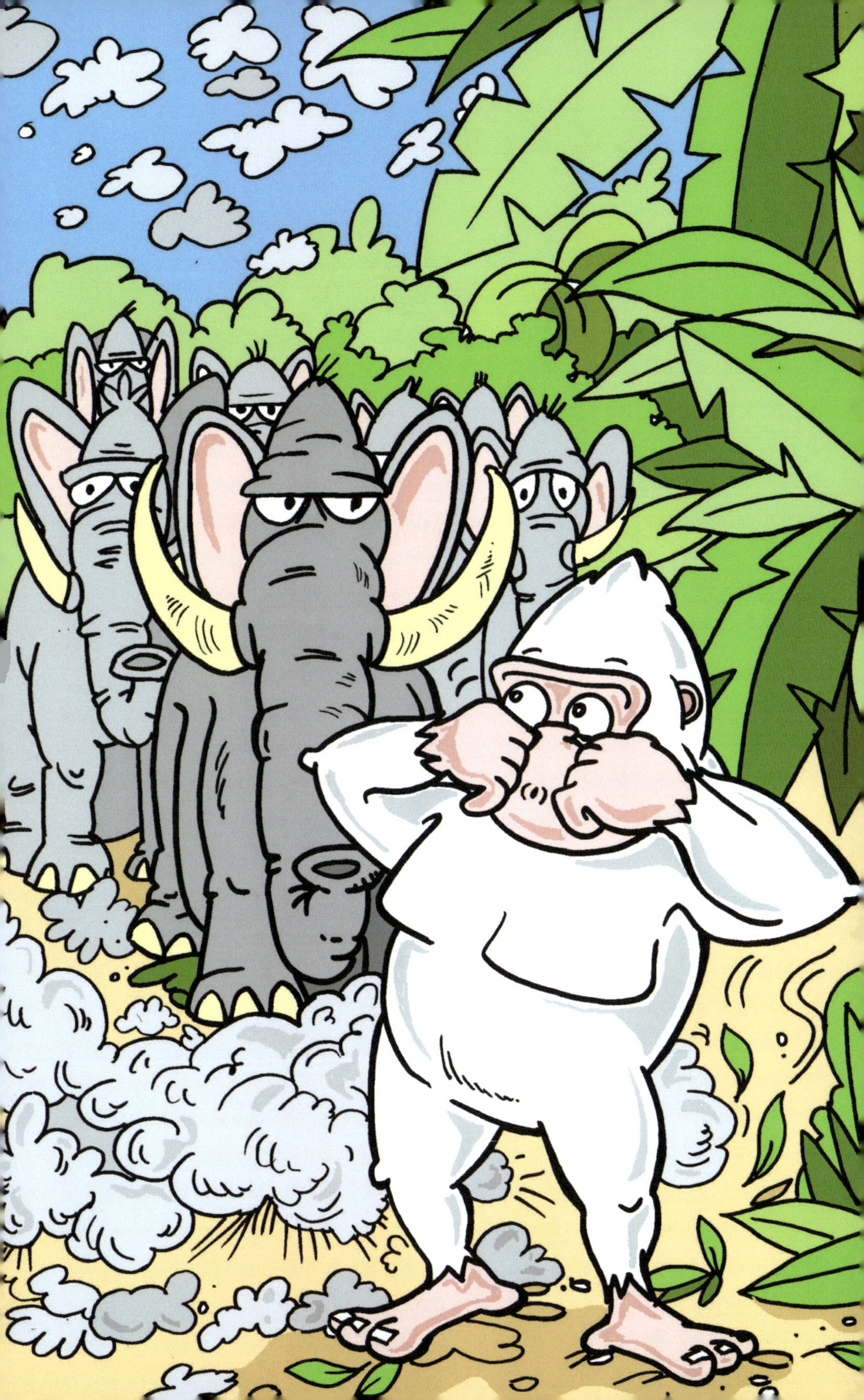

The elephants came to a halt in front of Snowflake.

'Can you help me, please?' he asked them.

'Of course, young Snowflake,' the grandfather elephant replied in his big, deep voice.

Snowflake was confused. 'How do you know my name?' he asked.

'You are the One – you will find the meaning of life,' a little voice replied from somewhere in the background.

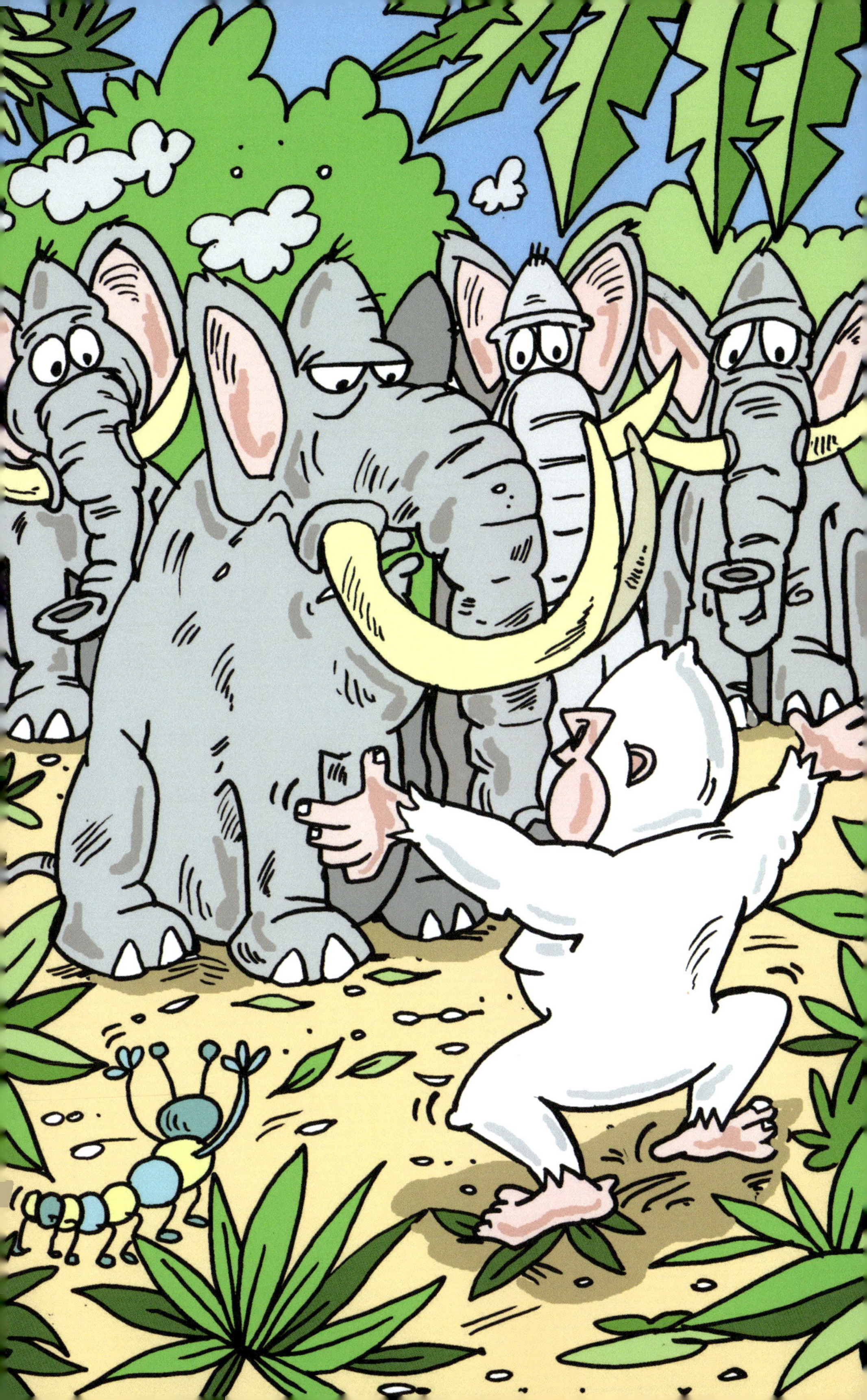

The owner of the little voice appeared from out of the bushes. It was Hope, Snowflake's friend from back home. 'I followed you so that if you got into any trouble, I could help,' Hope told Snowflake.

'Thank you!' Snowflake smiled. He was very pleased, as he was starting to feel lonely on his journey.

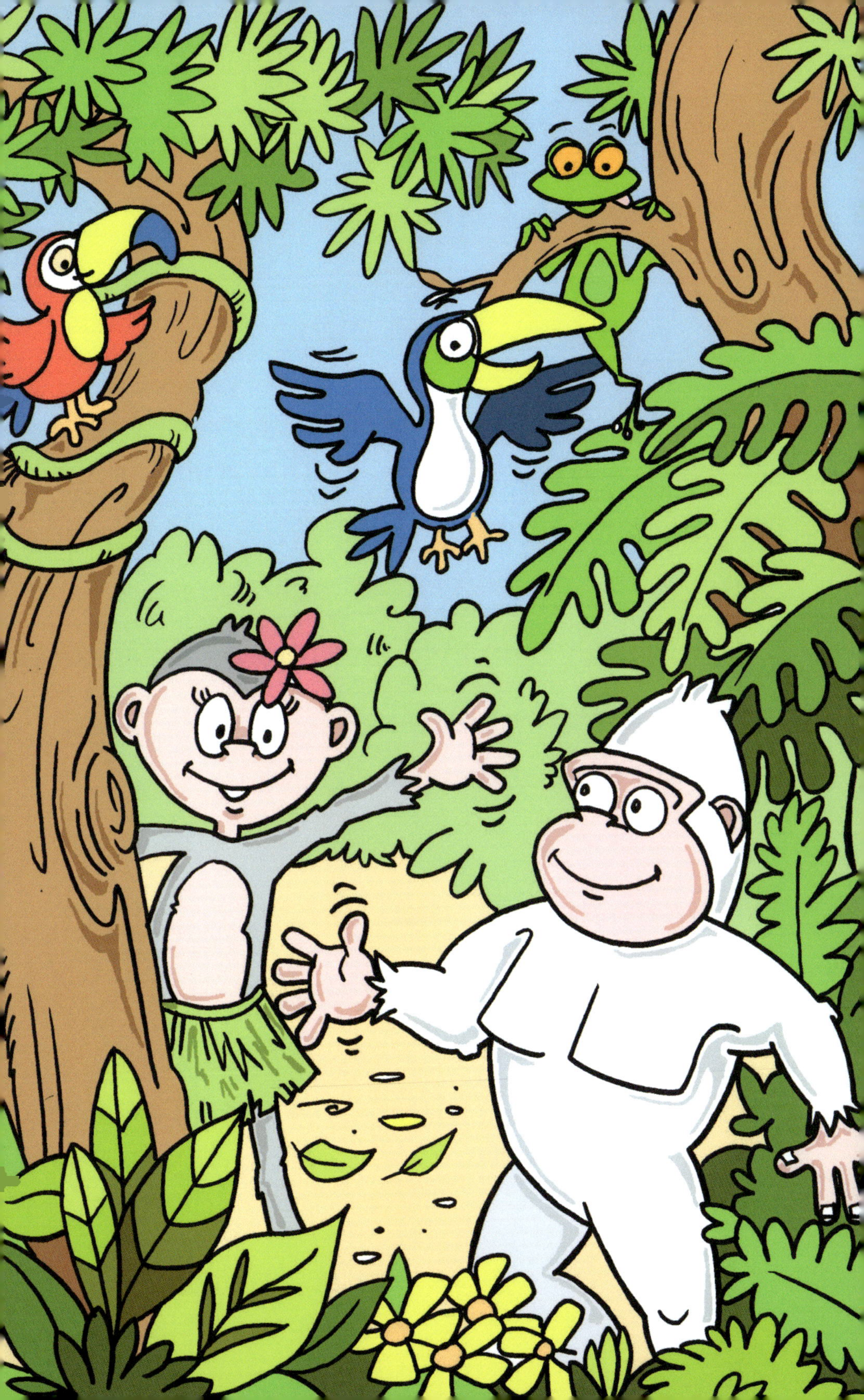

'How can we help you?' said the grandfather elephant kindly.

'The path to the top of Mount Lifelong splits into two, and I am not sure which one to take. Do you know which one is the best?' Snowflake asked.

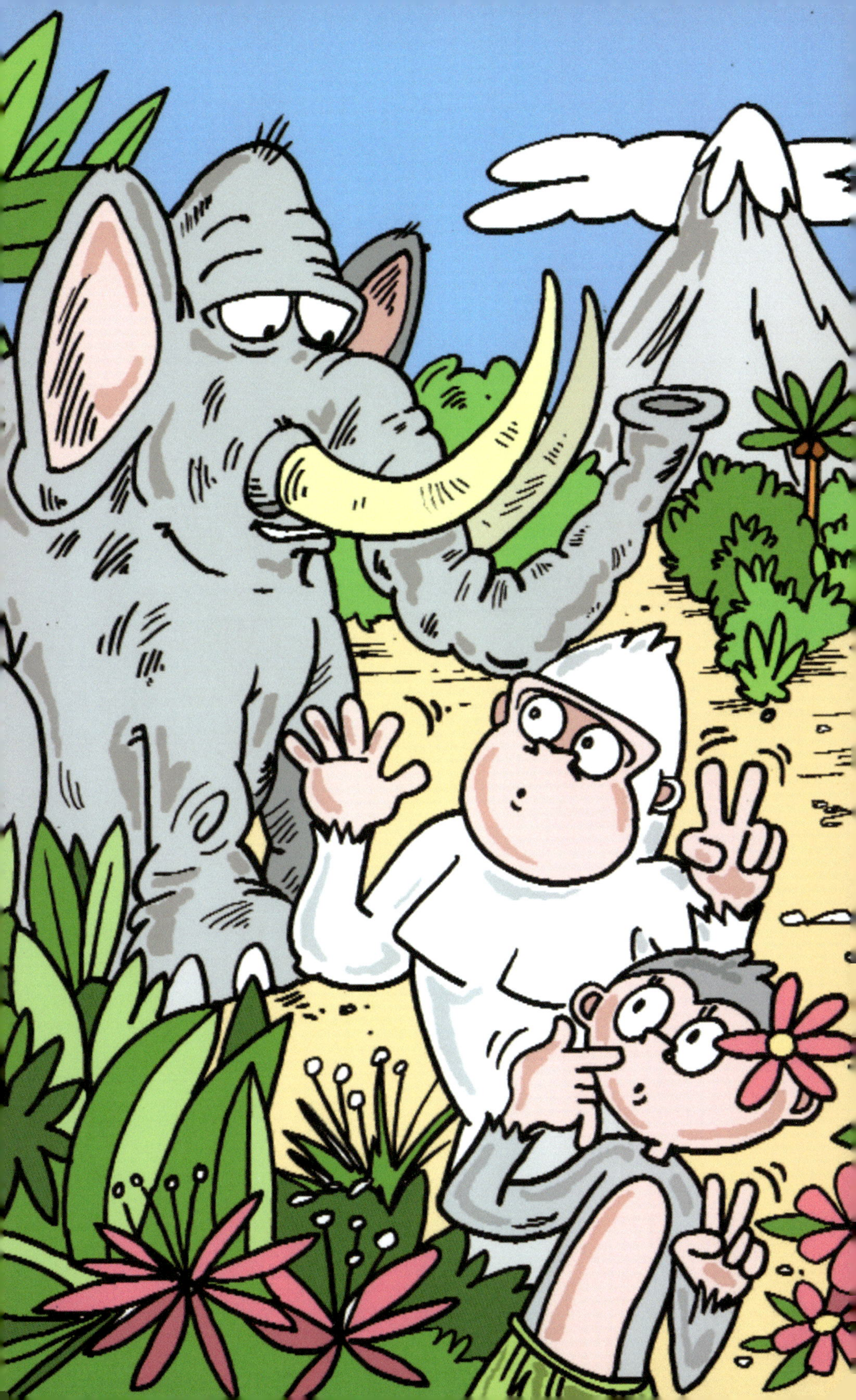

'I'm sorry, Snowflake – only you can decide that,' said the grandfather elephant.

'But how am I supposed to choose?' Snowflake asked, now very upset.

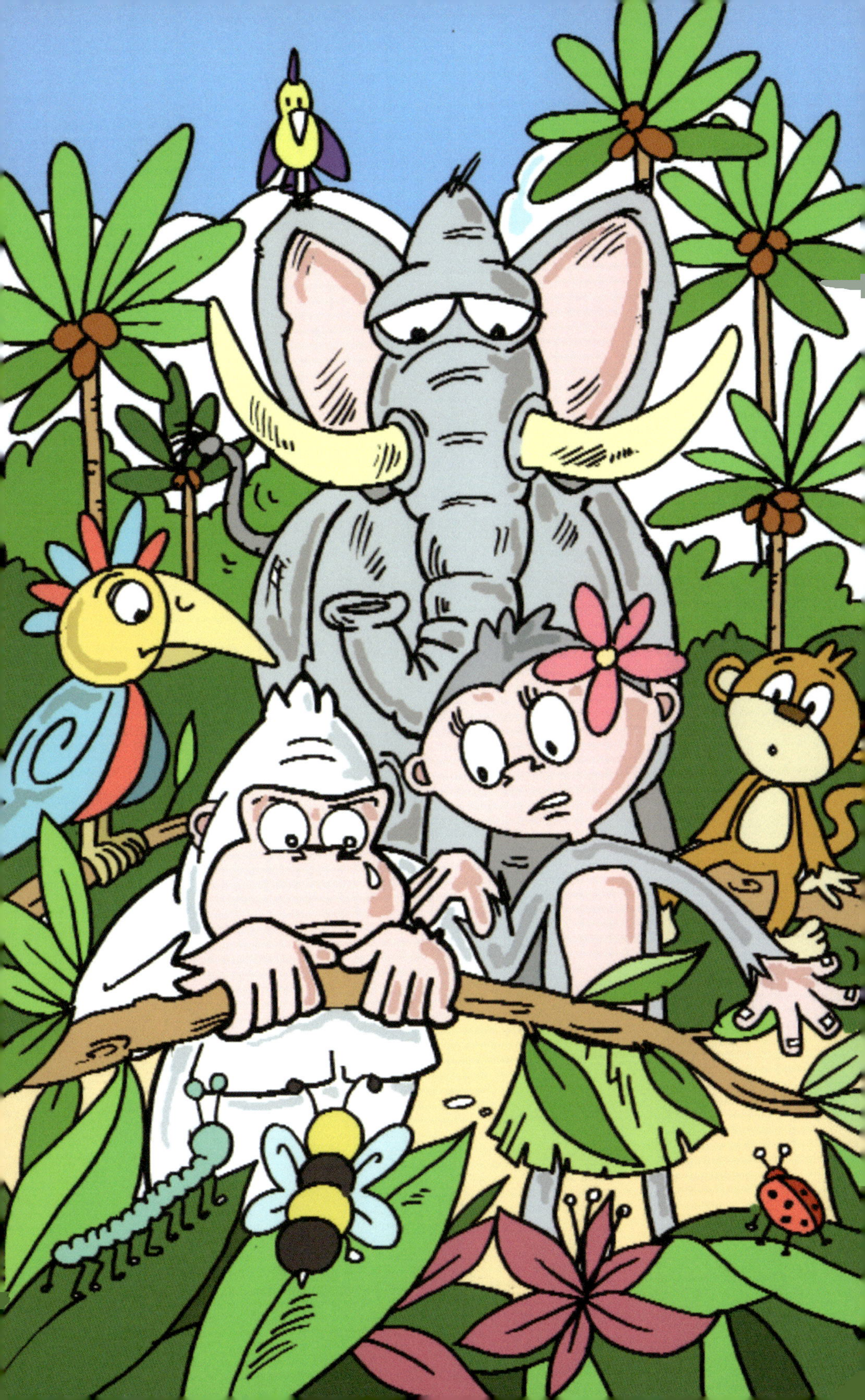

'You are the master of the Seven Sacred Movements. Use them to discover your path,' answered the wise old elephant.

As if a light had switched on in his head, Snowflake realised at once what he needed to do.

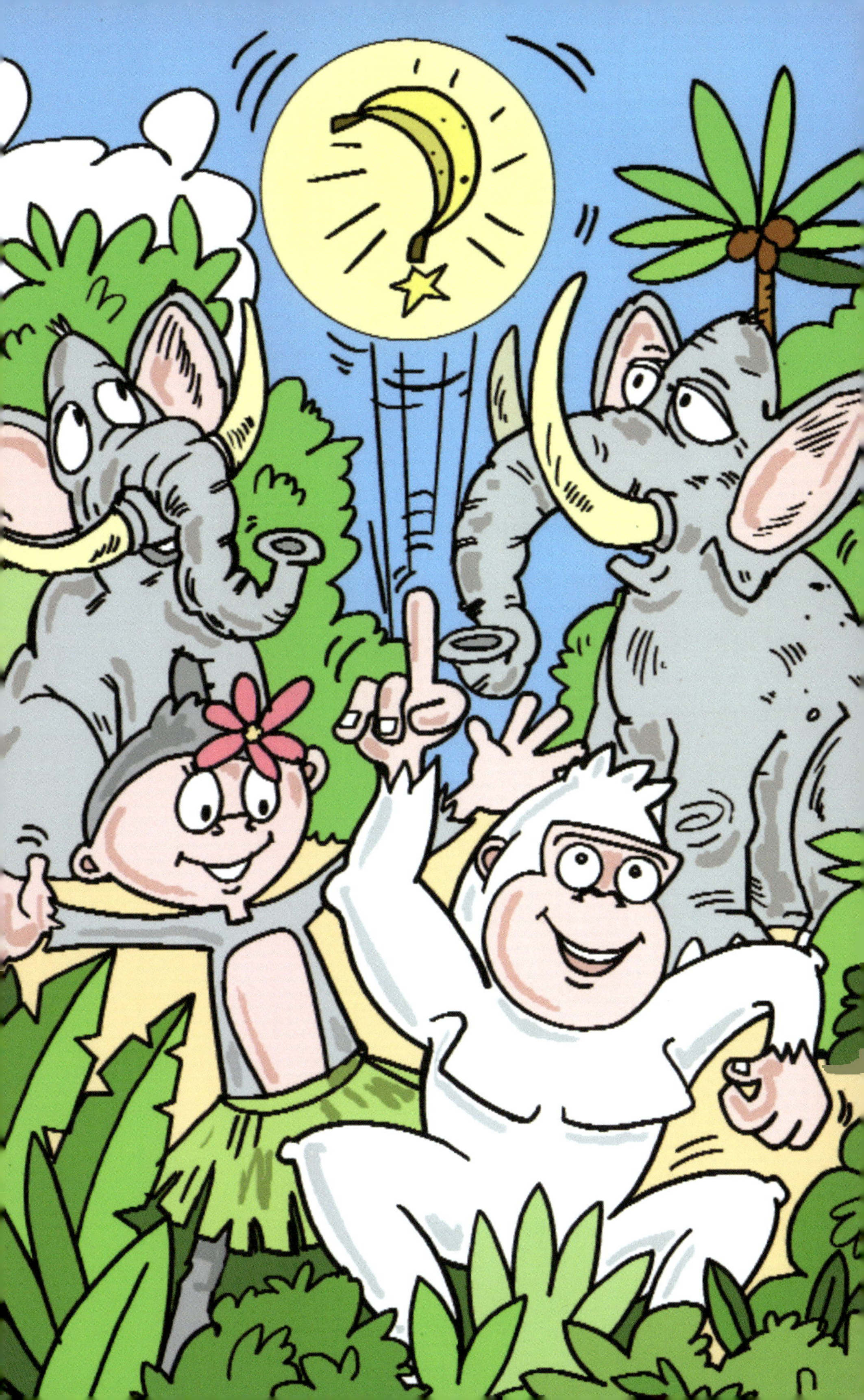

Snowflake sat in the **Silent Squat** position with Hope by his side. He began to focus his attention on his heart, whispering the words: 'Which direction does my heart wish to follow?' over and over to himself.

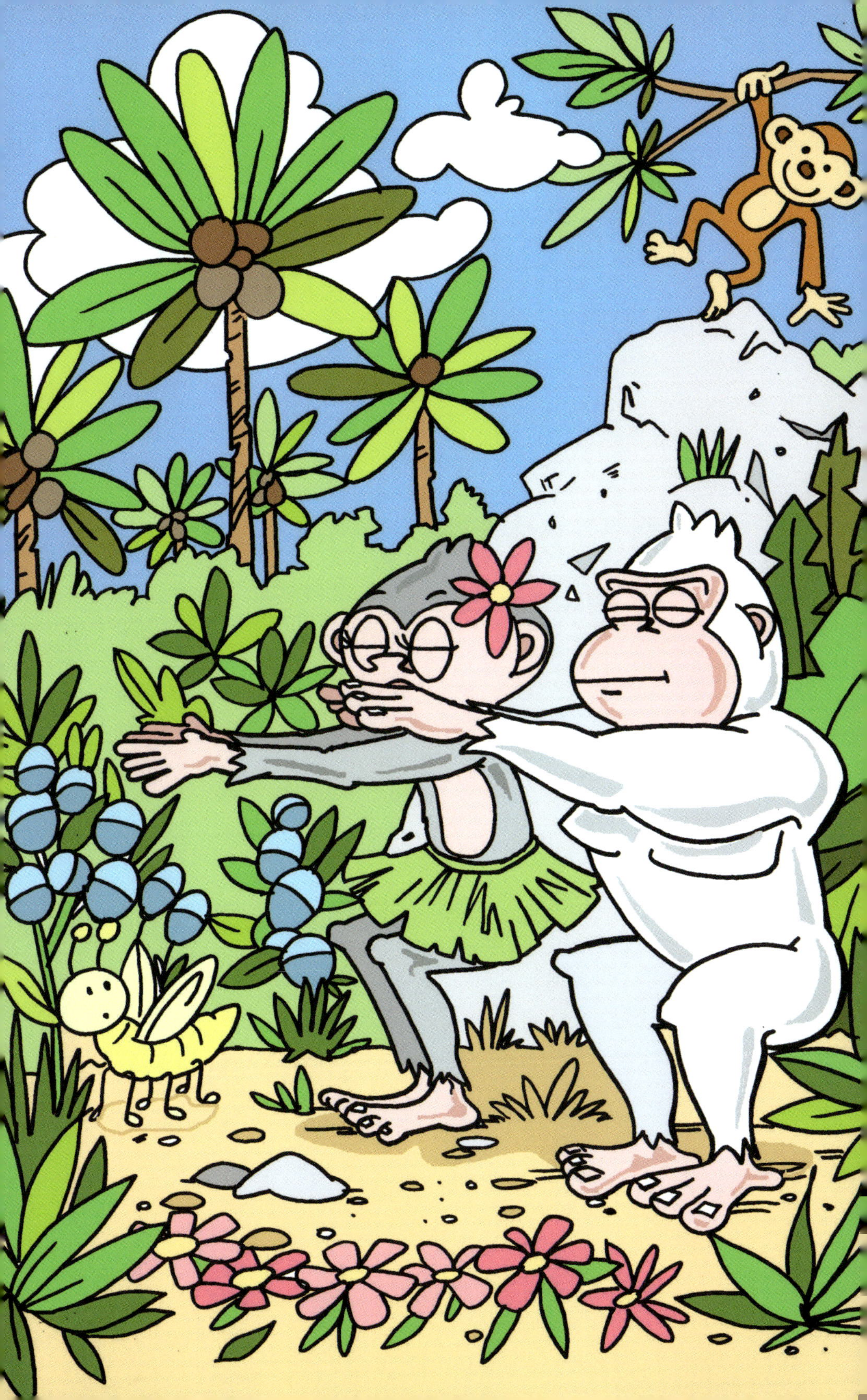

As clear as the blue skies above, the answer arrived. Snowflake now knew the direction his heart wanted to follow. 'Come on, Hope – let's go!' he said confidently.

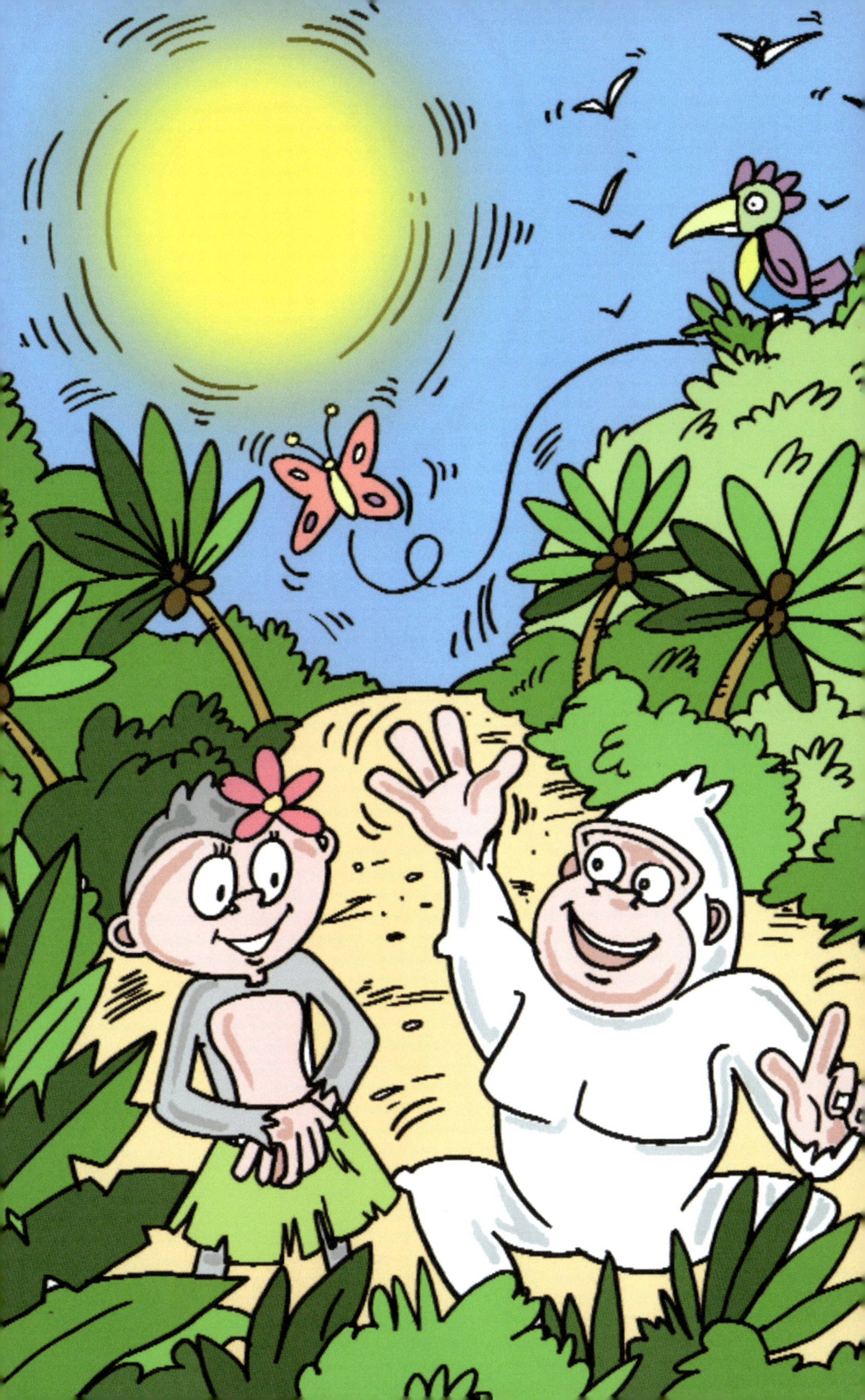

Soon after Snowflake and Hope began to follow the path towards the top of Mount Lifelong, they both became very hungry. Snowflake looked around for food but all he could find was a majestic berry tree.

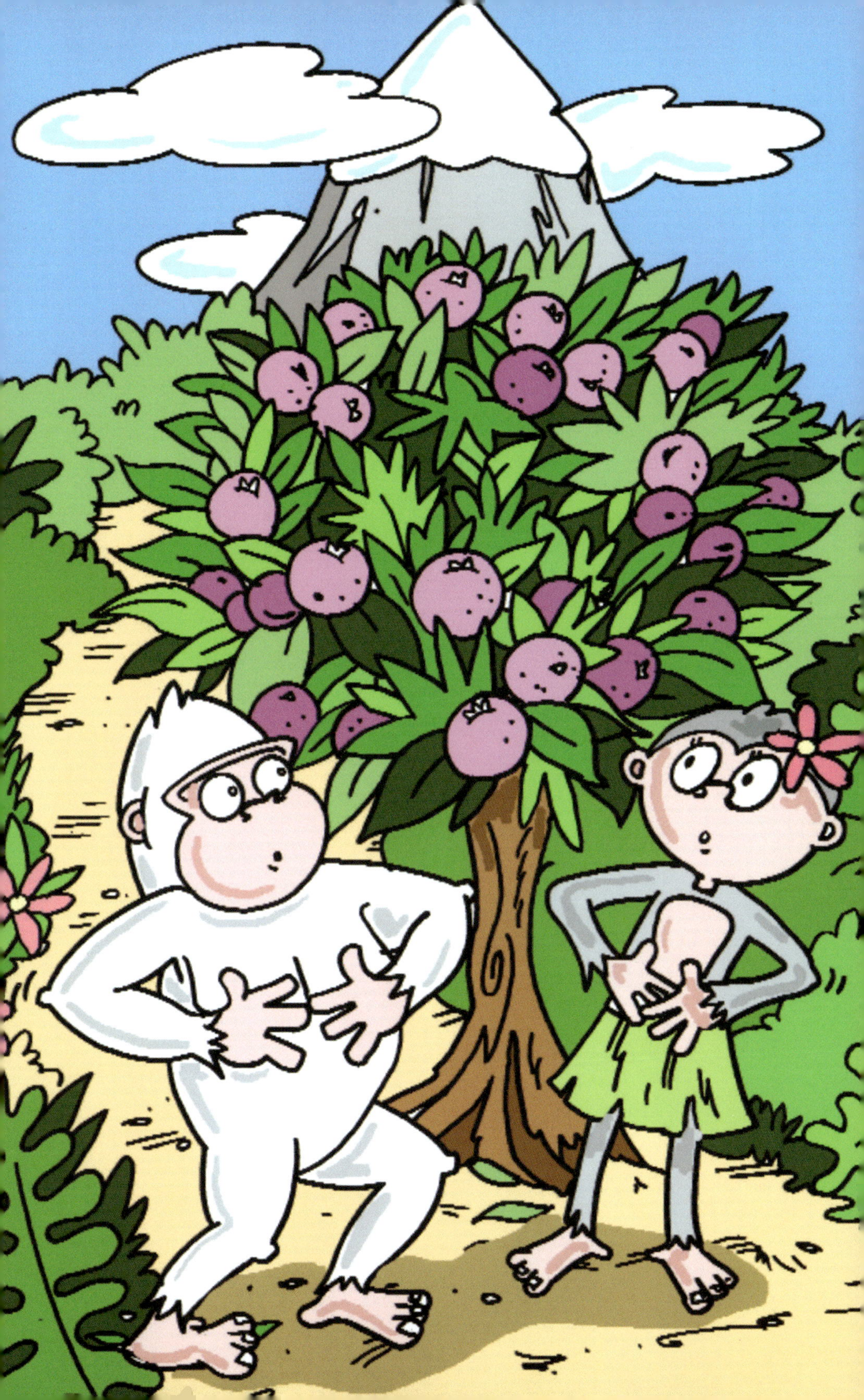

'We are forbidden to eat from those trees, Snowflake,' Hope said, feeling very cross.

'But it might be all we can find for miles, Hope,' Snowflake replied.

Just then, from the top of the tree, a sneaky snake appeared. 'Hello. My name is Pedro the Python,' it hissed.

Hello?

'Try my lovely majestic berries – they are so tasty,' Pedro whispered, slithering towards them.

Snowflake looked at Hope uncertainly – she seemed mesmerized by Pedro's voice. But the majestic berries did look very tempting.

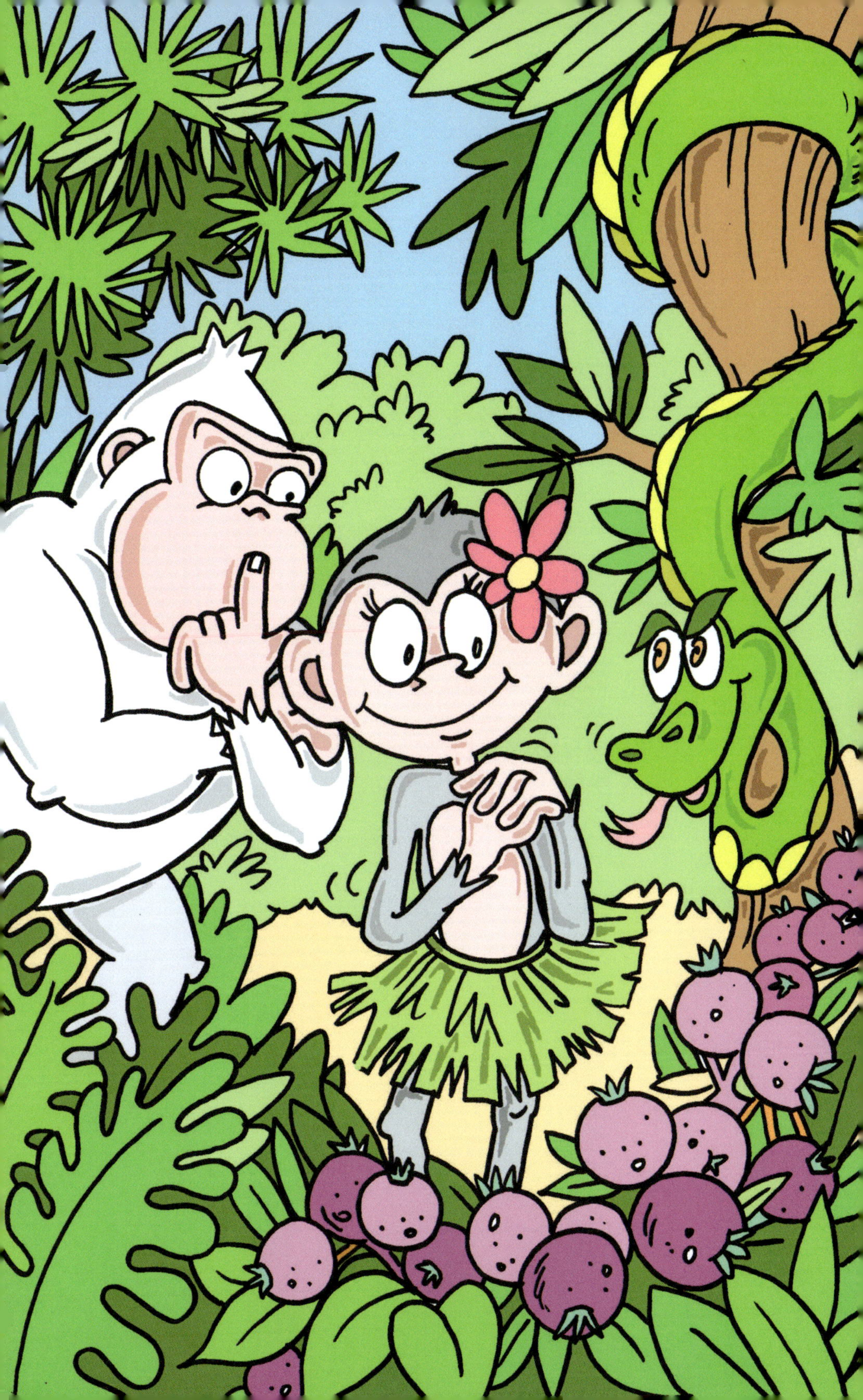

Snowflake turned away to take hold of a bunch of berries, not noticing that Pedro was now wrapping his body around Hope's legs, getting tighter and tighter all the while …

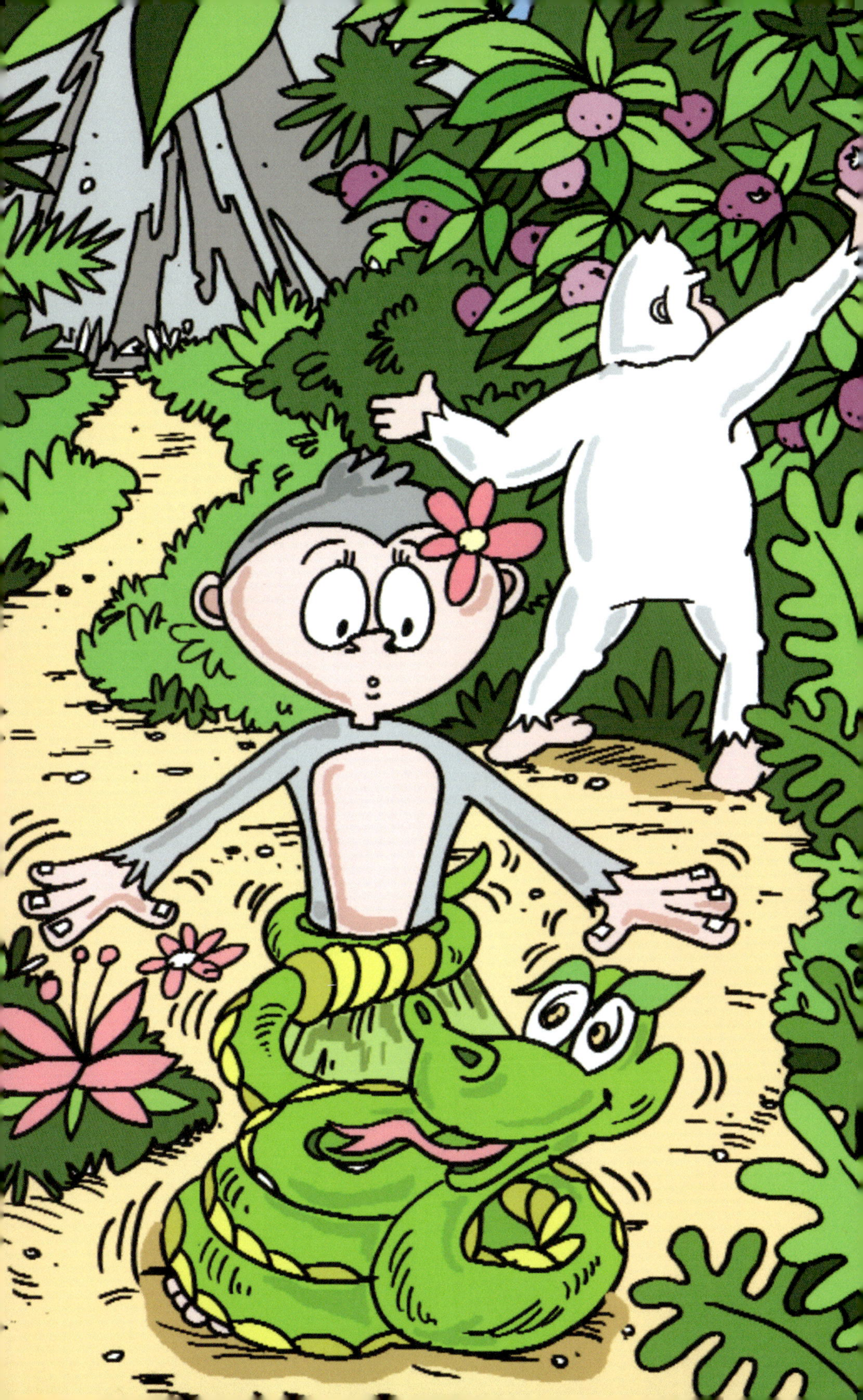

'Wait a second!' Snowflake jumped out of his trance, knowing what he needed to do. Using the **Limitless Lunge** to see past mistakes, Snowflake's mind travelled back through his memories. He remembered that Pedro had tried to trick him into eating the forbidden fruit of the tree once before, when he was a very young gorilla.

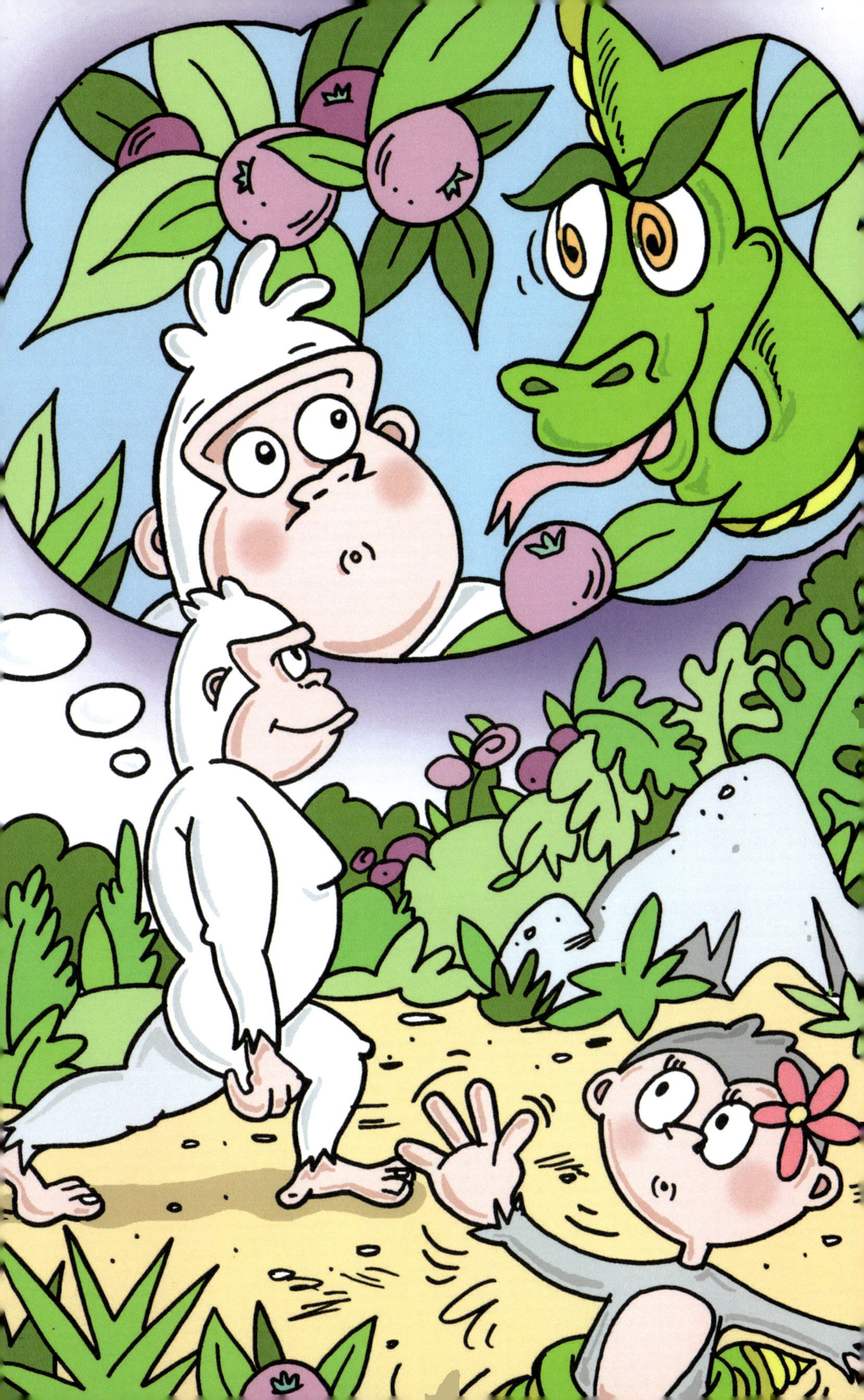

Back in the present moment, Snowflake turned and grabbed Hope from Pedro's clutches. 'Get away!' Snowflake roared.

Hope awoke from her trance. Shocked, she jumped on to Snowflake's back and they ran away from Pedro the sneaky snake.

'I'll get you one day!' Pedro hissed.

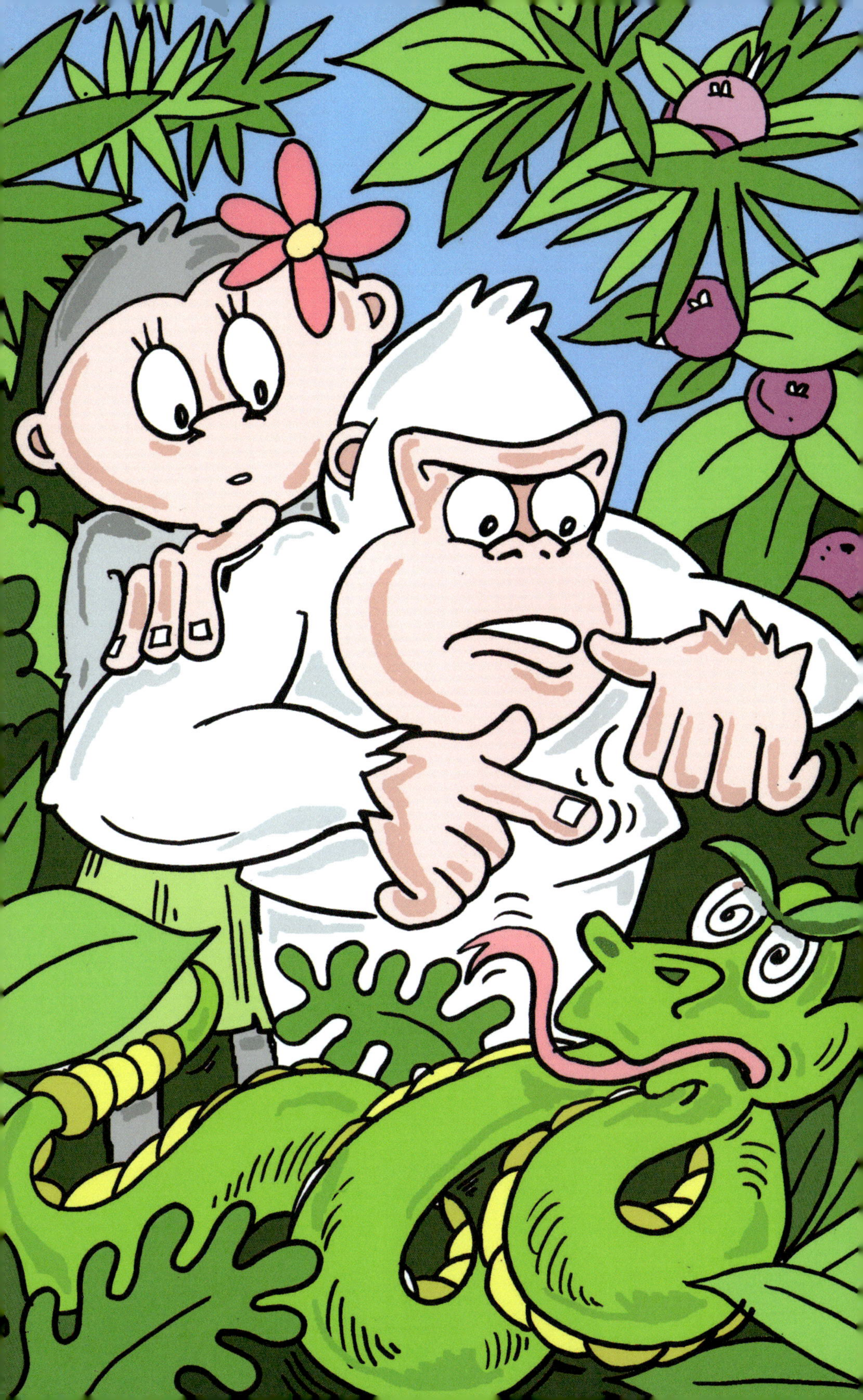

Now far along the mountain path, Snowflake and Hope found food and shelter for the night near River Rose. Snowflake gathered a bunch of bananas, and the two friends sat gazing at the stars.

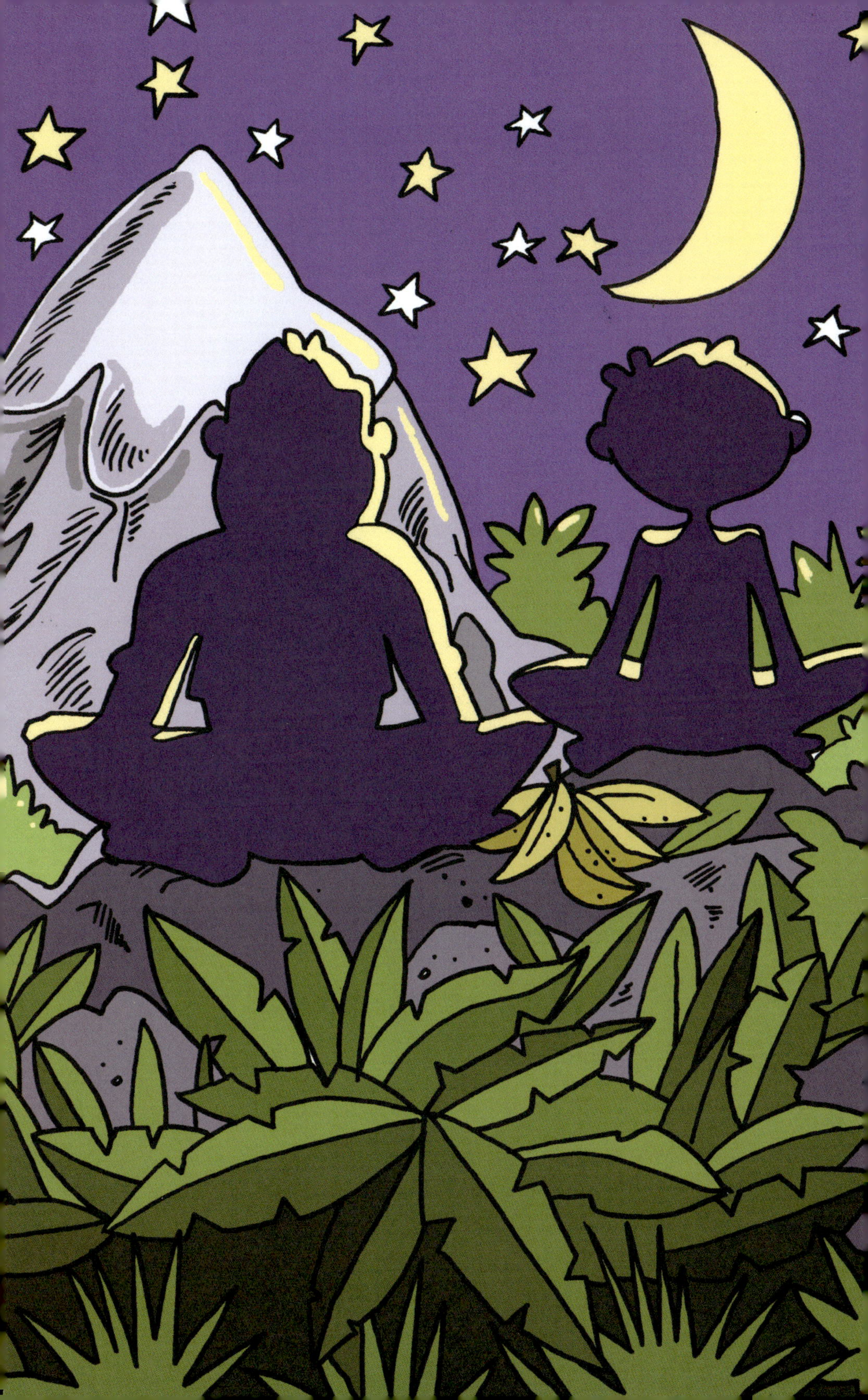

Hope turned to Snowflake. 'Will we ever get to the top of Mount Lifelong?' she asked.

'Of course we will,' Snowflake replied, as quick as a flash.

'What makes you so sure?' Hope asked curiously.

'Because we are together – and together we can do anything!' Snowflake smiled.

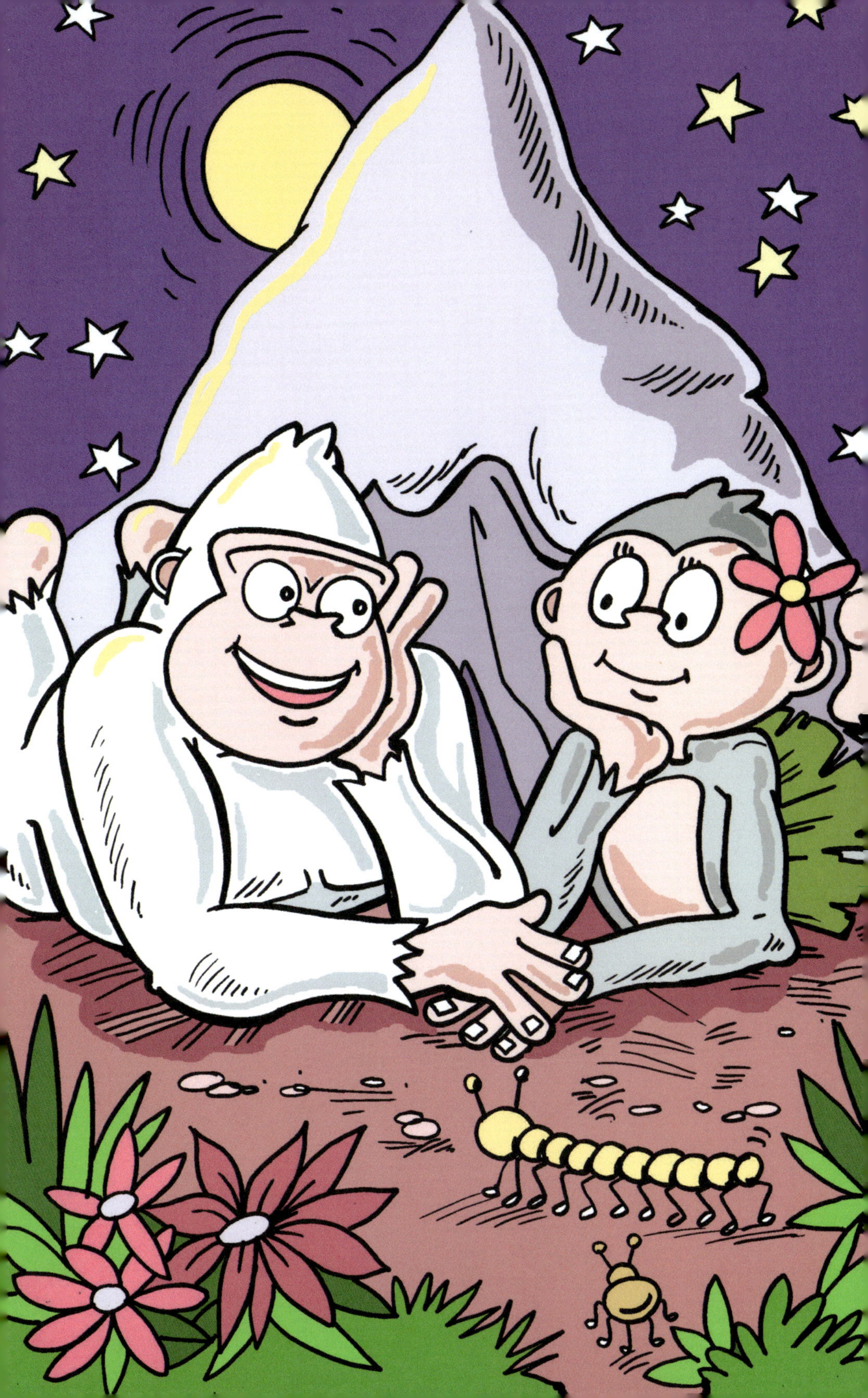

Chapter Three

Snowflake and Hope Meet the White Tiger

The sun had set, and Snowflake and Hope had come to a dead end on their path. In front of them was a gigantic rock, which was blocking the path to the top of Mount Lifelong.

'I don't understand,' Snowflake said. 'I used the **Silent Squat** to focus and listen to my heart – it told me to come this way.

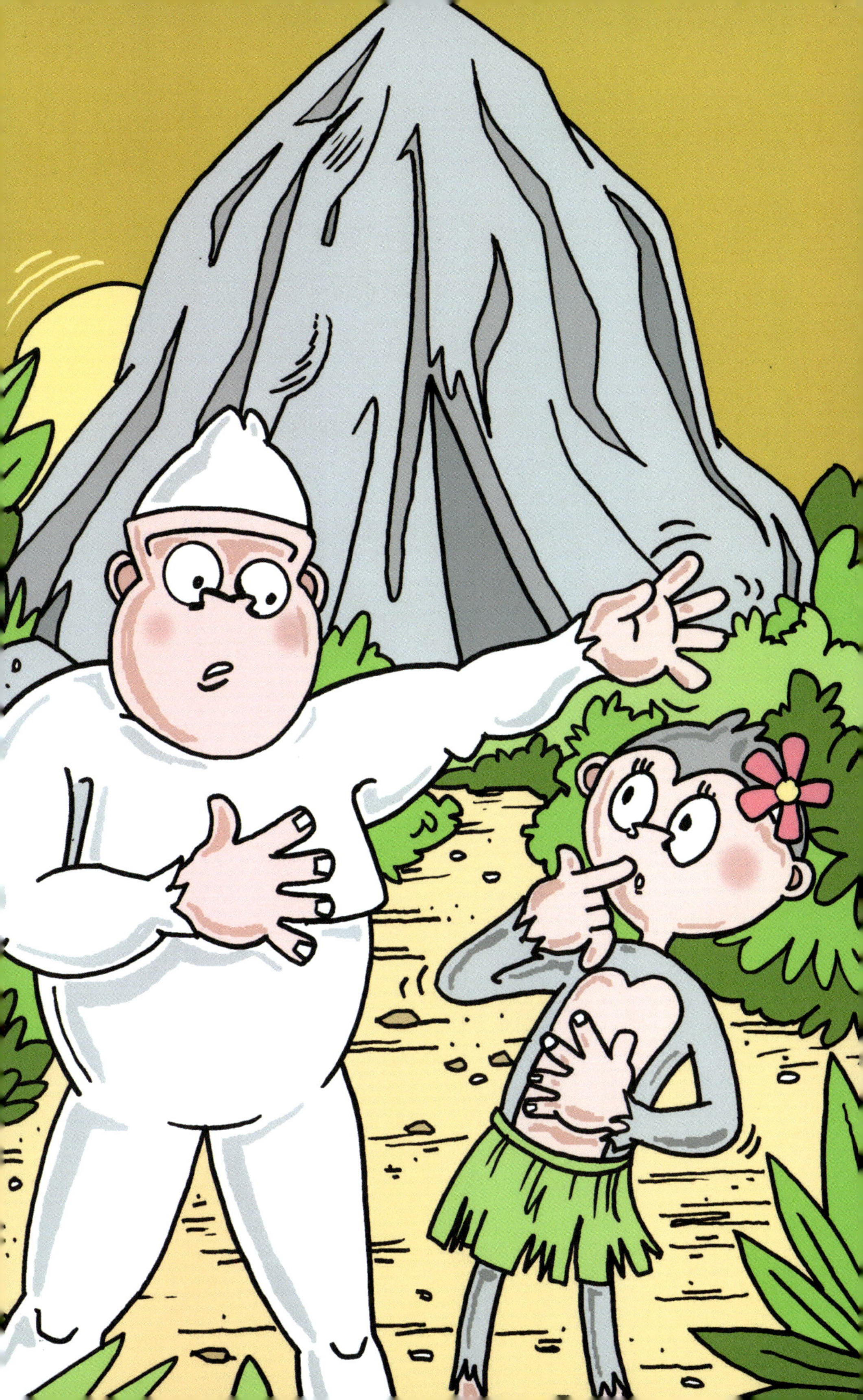

'Are you sure there is nothing we can do to move it?' Hope asked Snowflake.

Disheartened, Snowflake bowed his head. 'No, Hope. We will have to turn back, I'm afraid,' he said sadly.

Just then, a gust of wind came drifting by, carrying a faint echo. 'You are stronger than you think! Look within,' it whispered.

Snowflake listened to the echo thoughtfully. Suddenly, he jumped up. 'The **Powerful Push**!' he shouted.

you are *stronger* than you think

Snowflake had remembered the Seven Sacred Movements. He began to focus his energy, letting it flow from his heart and using the **Powerful Push** against the gigantic rock. Before long, the rock began to move.

'You're doing it, Snowflake!' Hope shouted joyfully.

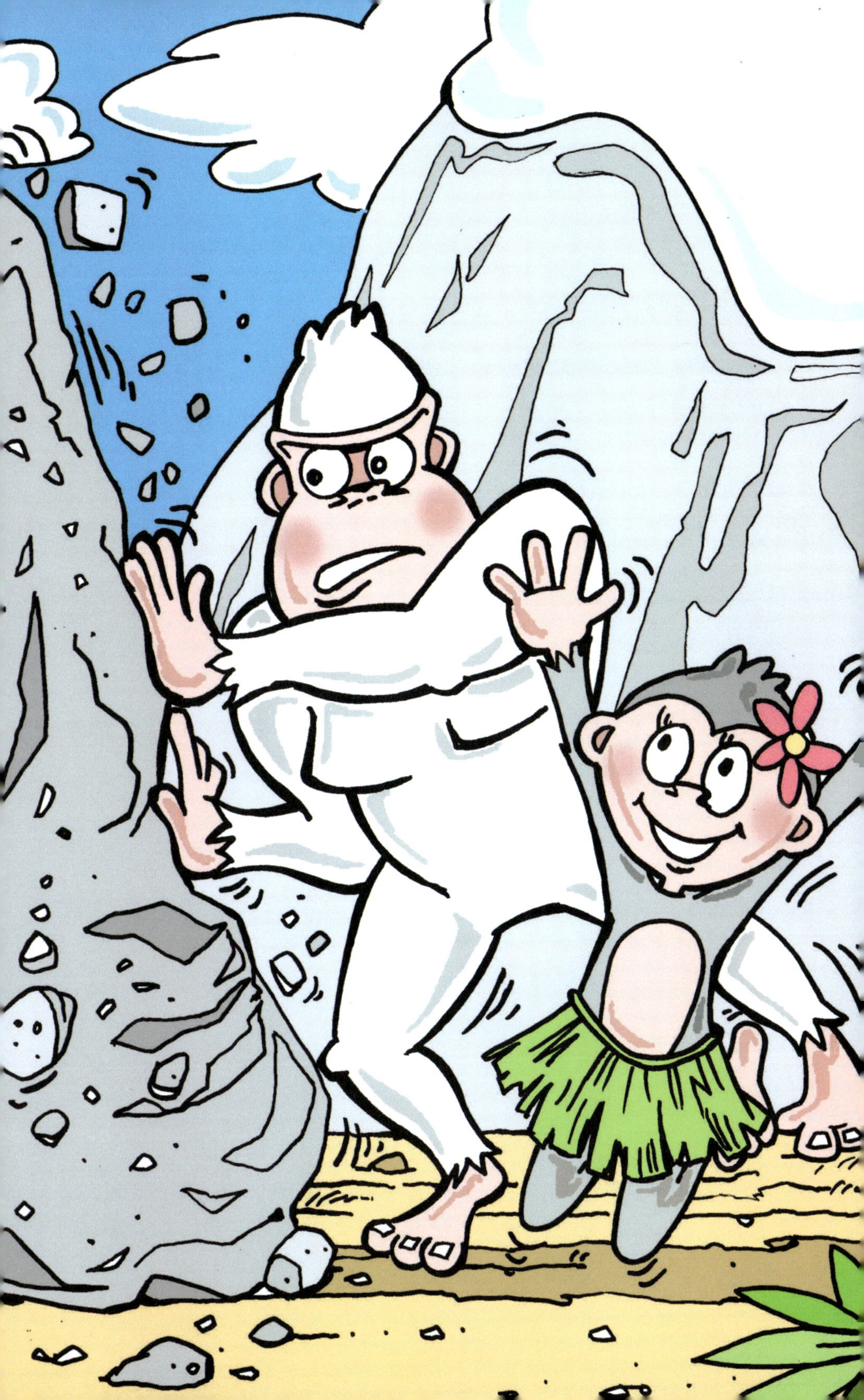

As Snowflake pushed the gigantic rock out of the way, the path to the top of Mount Lifelong was revealed. But moving the rock had caused an avalanche of smaller rocks to fall from the mountain, and these were now tumbling down the path. Snowflake was so tired that he could hardly move.

'Come on, Snowflake – we are going to get crushed!' Hope said desperately.

Snowflake then remembered what Charlie the silverback had taught him:

'If we push, we must always pull – this is the balance'.

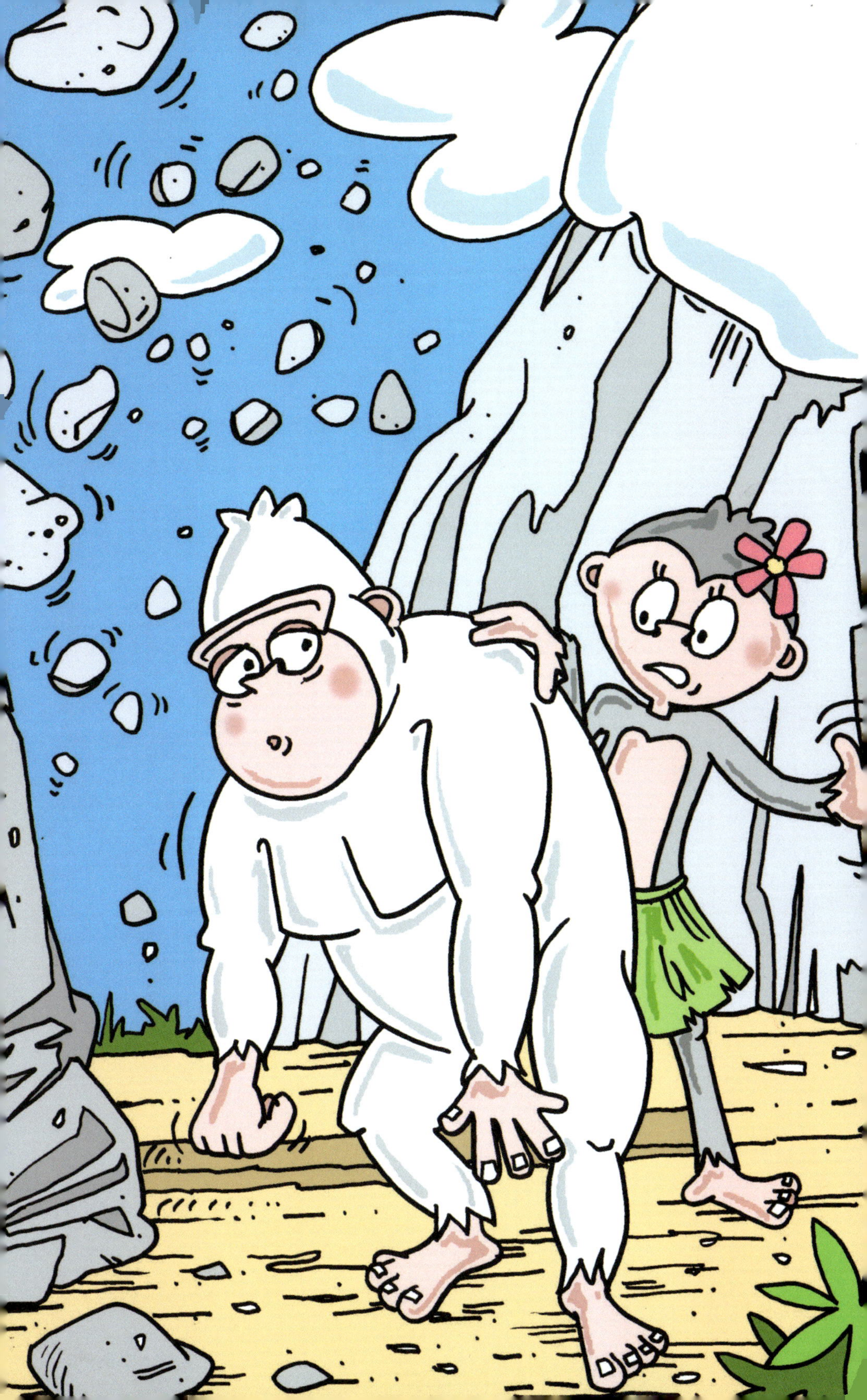

Snowflake started the **Peaceful Pull** to restore his energy. It came back so fast that he moved like a rocket. 'Come on, Hope – there's no time to waste!' he shouted as he jumped to his feet. On they went up Mount Lifelong.

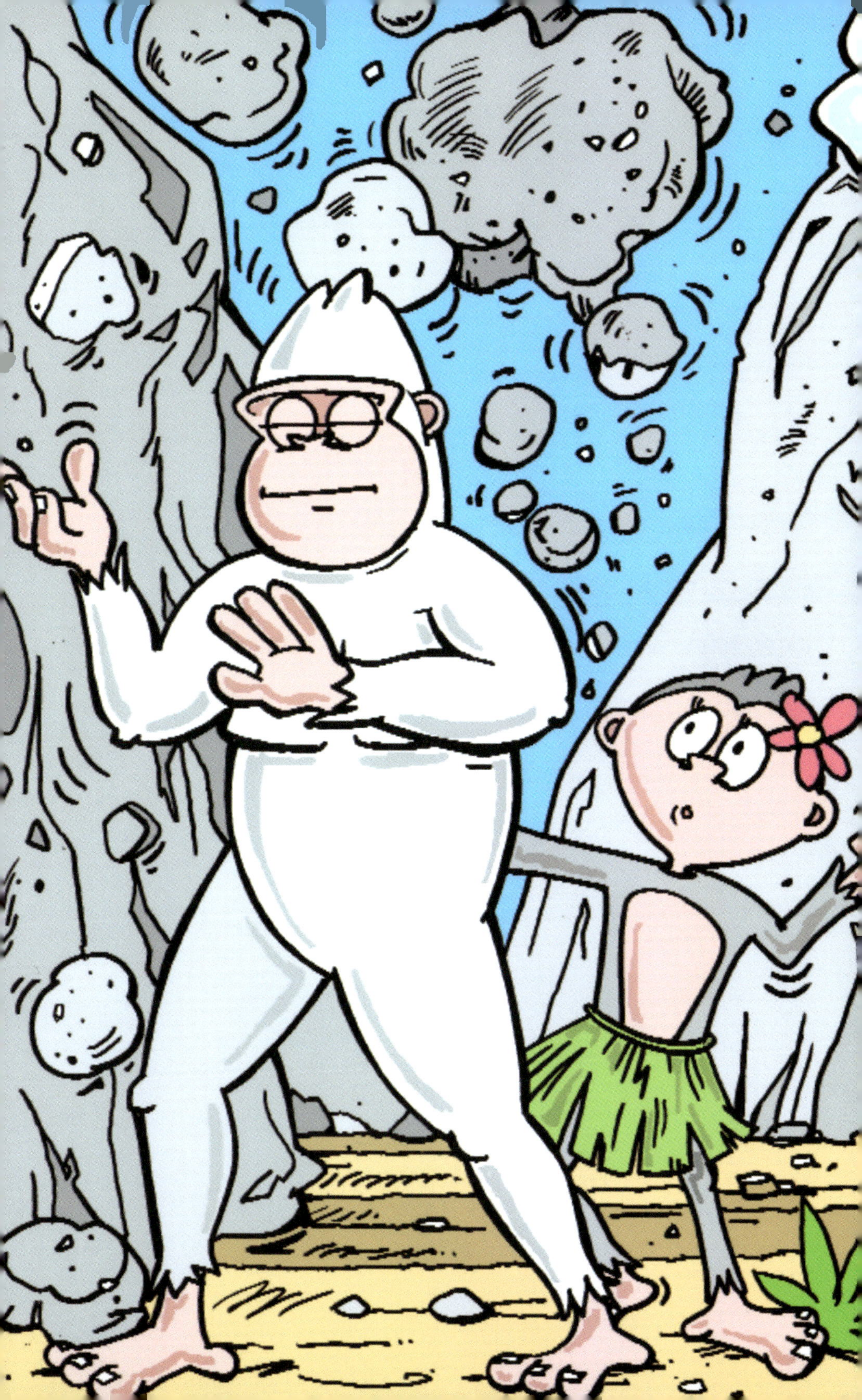

Snowflake and Hope were near the end of the path and were almost at the top of Mount Lifelong when they heard a noise up ahead. 'Help!' they heard as they got closer. Snowflake ran towards the noise. He could see something stuck under a fallen tree.

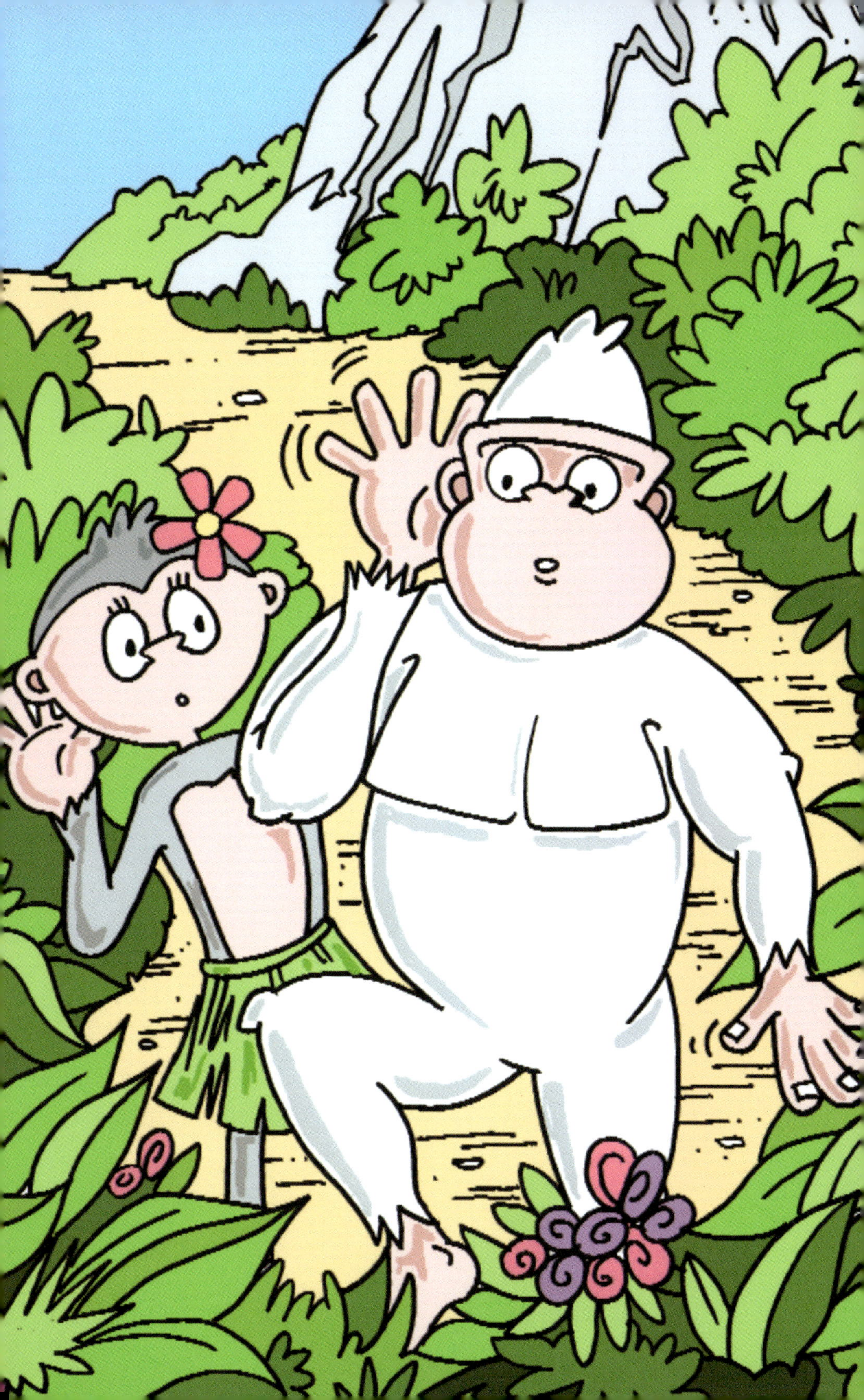

Under the tree, they found a crazy crocodile.

'Please can you help me?' the crocodile wept.

'Snowflake, we have to help him!' said Hope. 'What is your name, crocodile?'

'My name is Callum,' the crocodile replied.

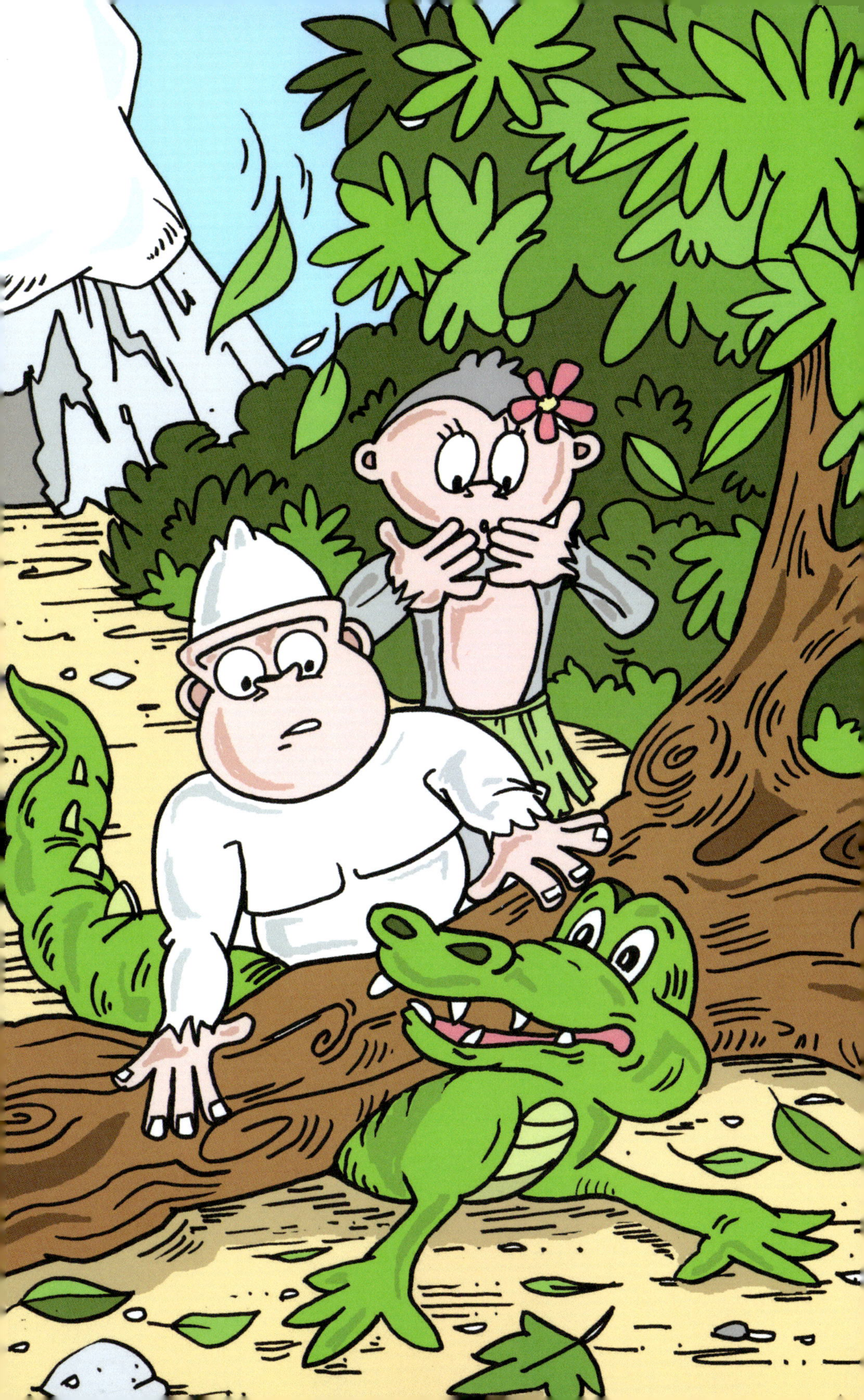

Snowflake thought as hard as he could about how he could rescue Callum. 'Aha!' he eventually burst out. 'The **Brave Bend** gives me the strength of ten gorillas!' He looked at the tree. 'Give me the strength to lift this tree,' he whispered, taking hold of the trunk.

Crash! The tree shifted, and Callum was finally free.

'Thank you!' Callum said with relief.

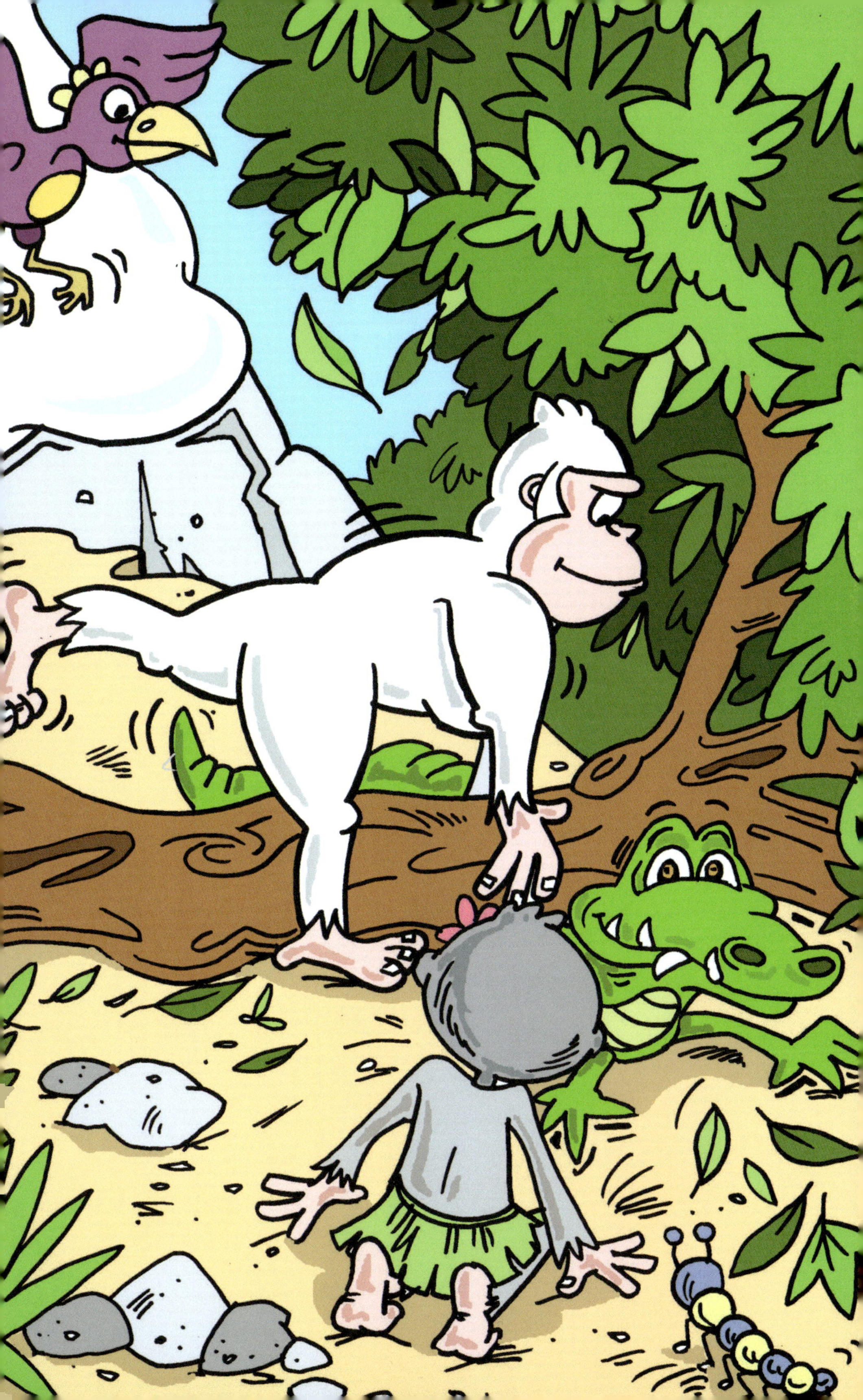

Snowflake and Hope were almost there – they could see the top of Mount Lifelong ahead of them. Then, all of a sudden, the sun went down and the mountain became very dark.

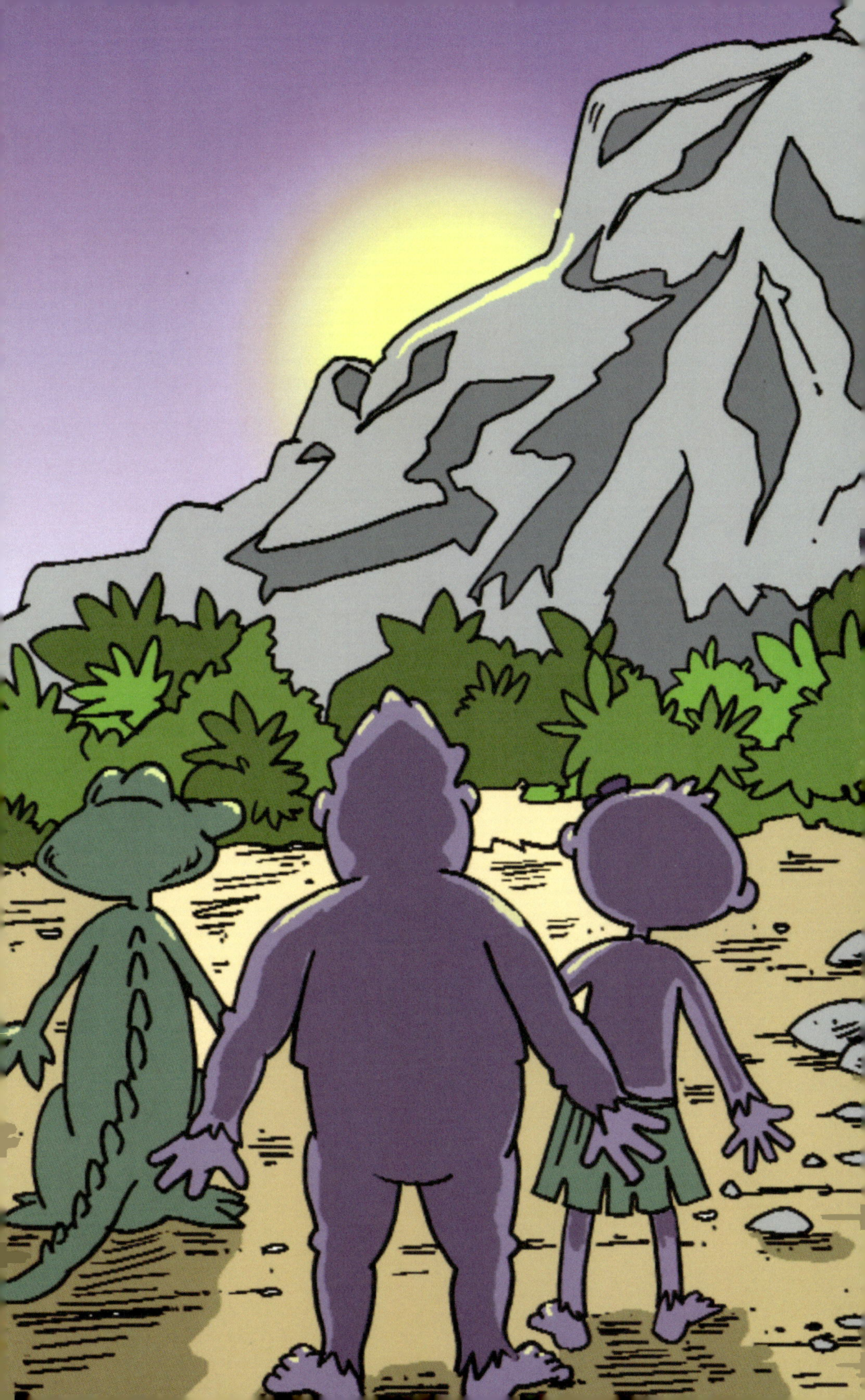

Hope was startled. 'Can I hold your hand?' she asked Snowflake.

'Of course,' Snowflake replied. 'But we must finish this journey,' he added, his voice full of determination.

Snowflake and Hope went on through the dark, until finally they realized that their passion and commitment had taken them to the top of Mount Lifelong.

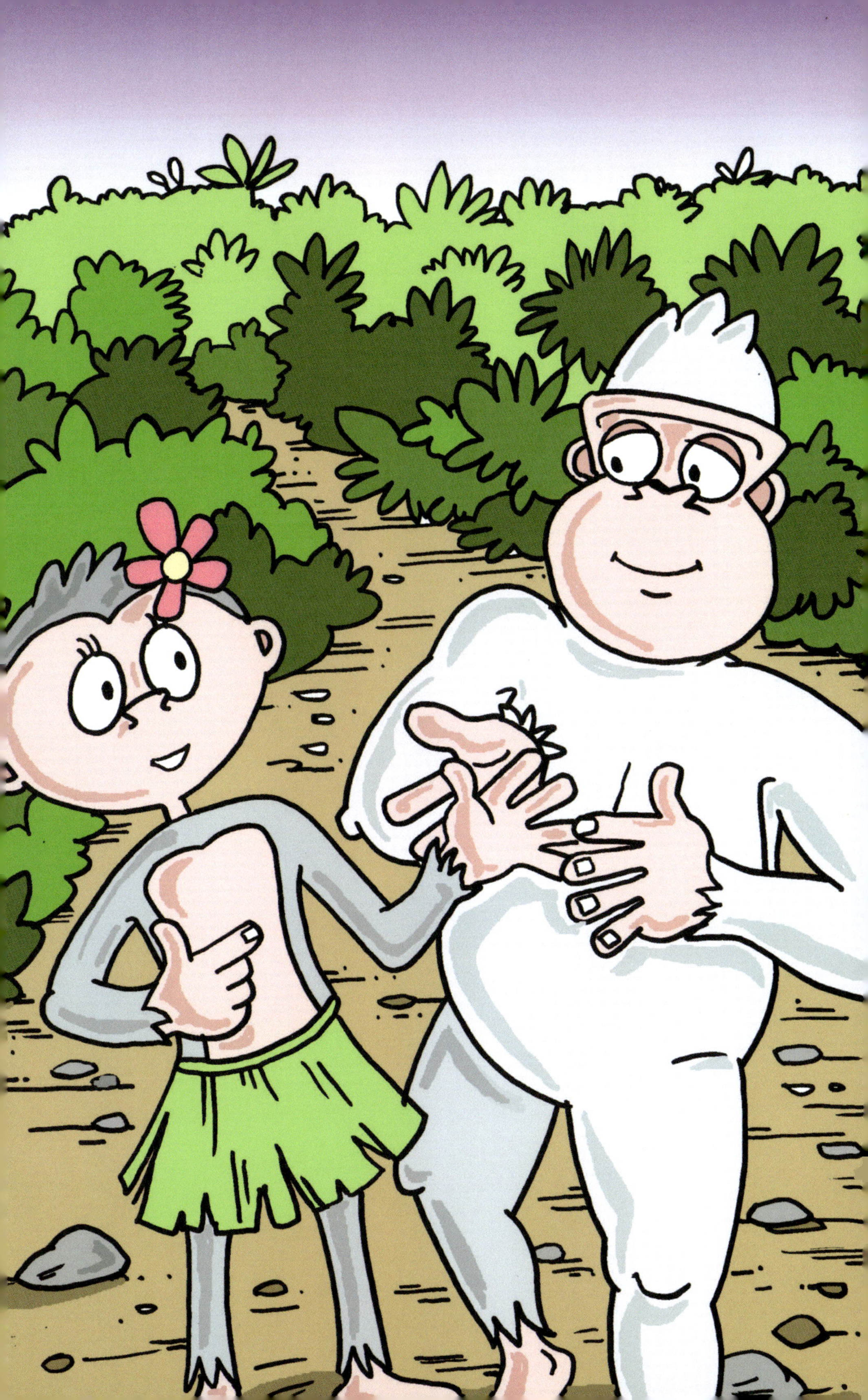

Snowflake and Hope were so excited that they had achieved their goal. However, after a moment or two, they realized that there was nothing to be seen – nothing except for an old statue of a White Tiger with some ancient writing on it.

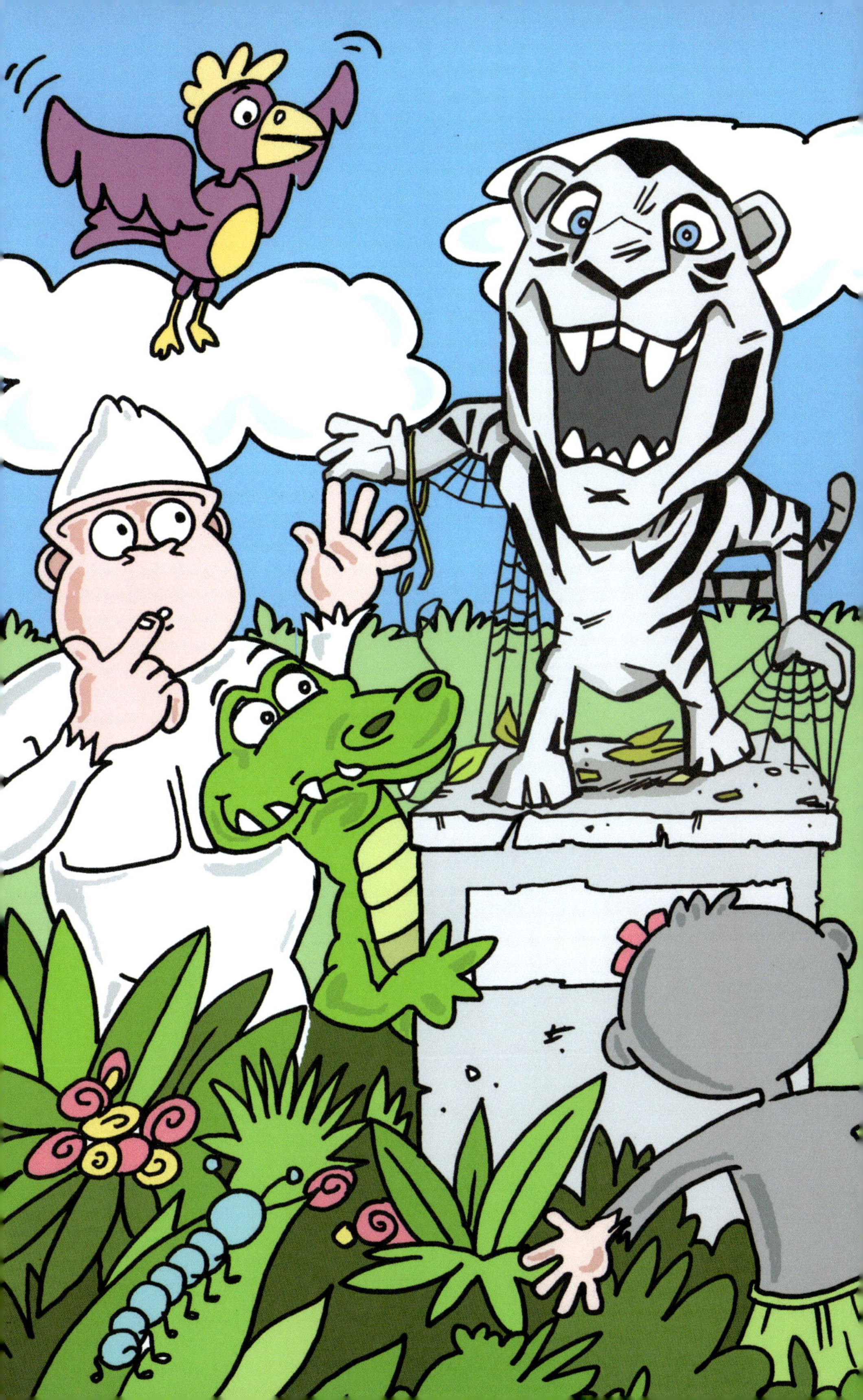

Ignite me and all will be revealed, read the writing on the statue.

Hope was confused. 'Where are we supposed to get fire from, all the way up here, Snowflake?'

Snowflake already knew the answer. He would need the **Tornado Twist** – the movement which controls all the elements.

IGNITE ME AND ALL WILL BE REVEALED

Snowflake began the **Tornado Twist**, focusing on bringing fire to life upon the statue. Hope was amazed at how focused Snowflake had become and how he had mastered the Seven Sacred Movements during their long journey.

IGNITE ME AND ALL WILL BE REVEALED

'Fire!' yelled Hope.

Snowflake had ignited the statue.

All of a sudden, white smoke surrounded Snowflake and Hope. The wind blew faster and faster, and the words 'Love, love, love …' were being whispered in the air.

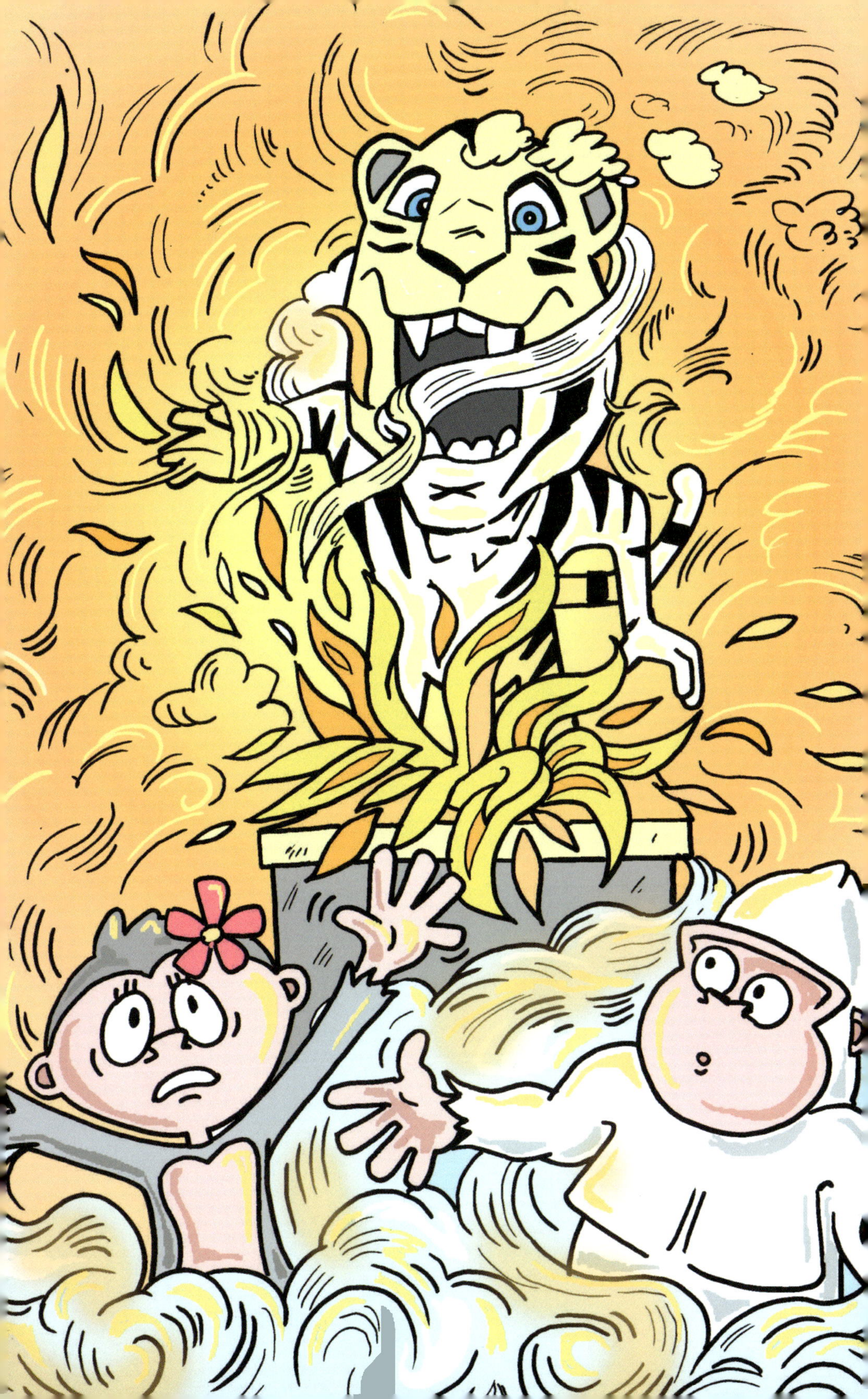

Out of the smoke, the White Tiger appeared. Snowflake and Hope were dazzled.

'So – you managed to get here, Snowflake?' the White Tiger said in his really cool voice.

'I did,' said Snowflake proudly. 'Can you tell me,' he continued politely, 'what is the meaning of life?'

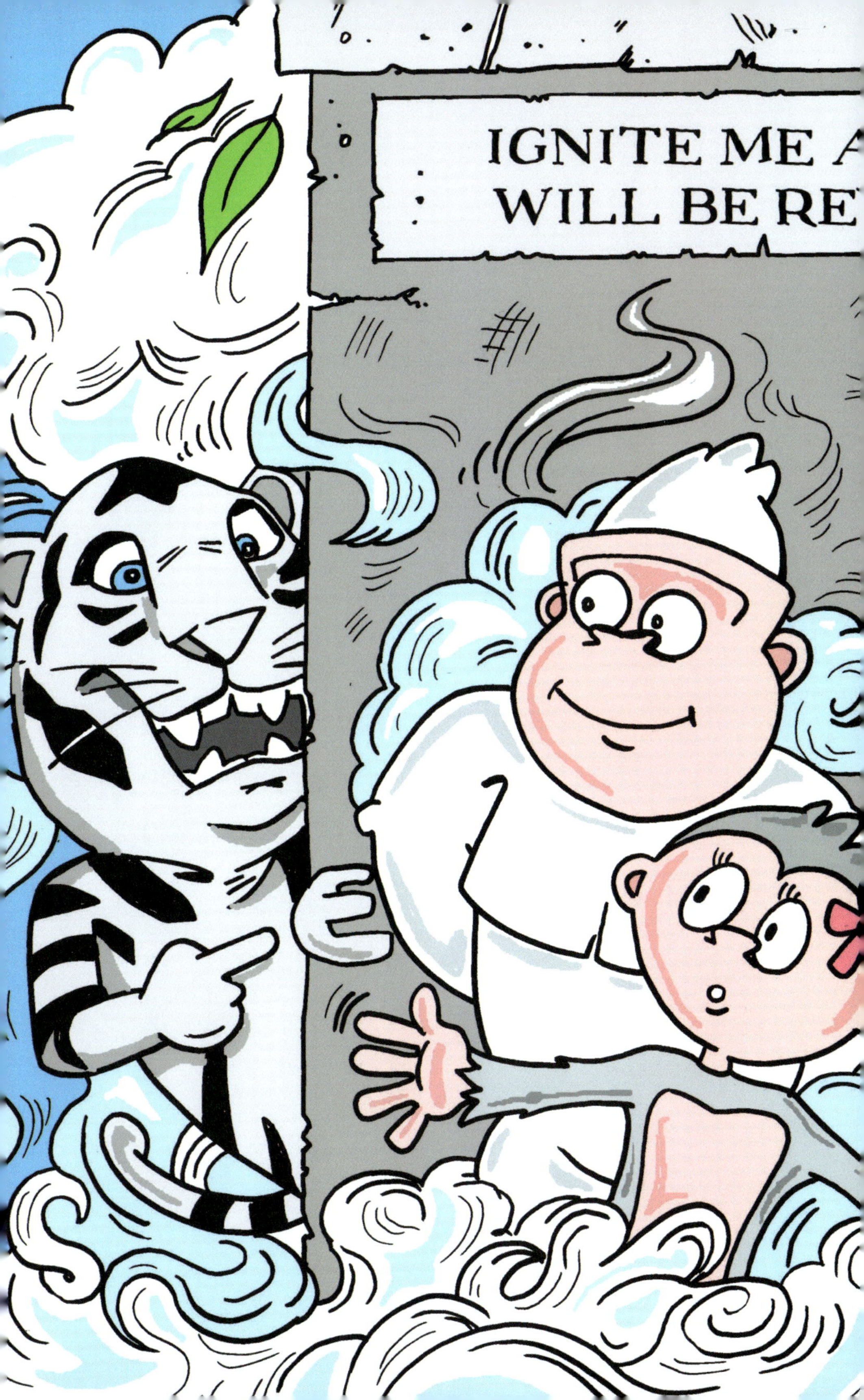
IGNITE ME A
WILL BE RE

'You know I can't tell you,' the White Tiger said in a mysterious voice. 'You must walk like me to discover such a secret.'

Snowflake knew that the **White Tiger Walk** was the last movement he had to master to reveal the meaning of life. The White Tiger began his walk.

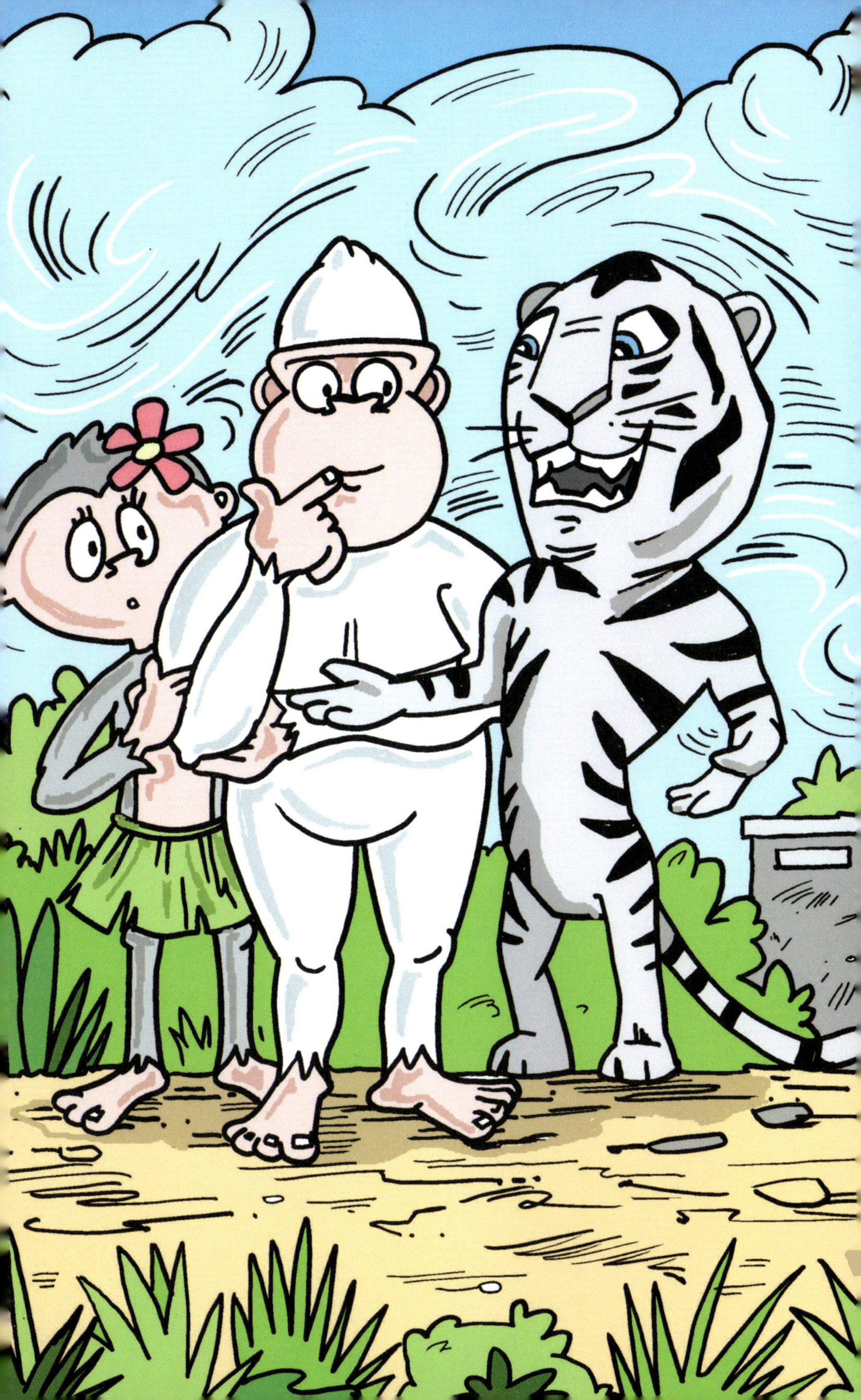

Hope sat and watched the magical moment between Snowflake and the White Tiger. She knew that life was about to change. Suddenly, the walk stopped and the White Tiger was ready to tell them the meaning of life.

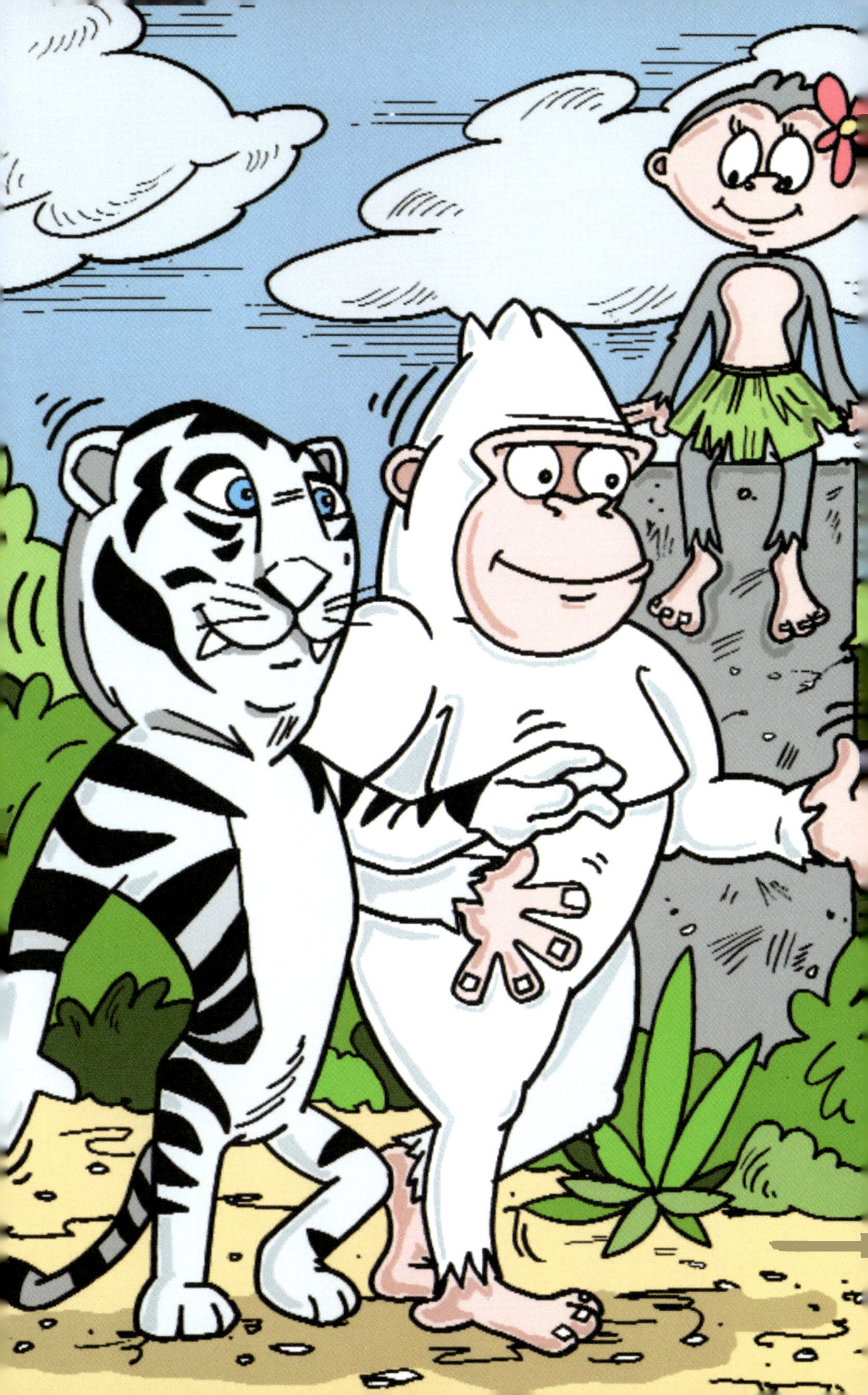

Snowflake took hold of Hope's hand as the White Tiger spoke:

'**The meaning of life ... is a life with meaning. This means listening to your heart, being grateful for the little things in life, and always loving life for what it is ... a gift**'.

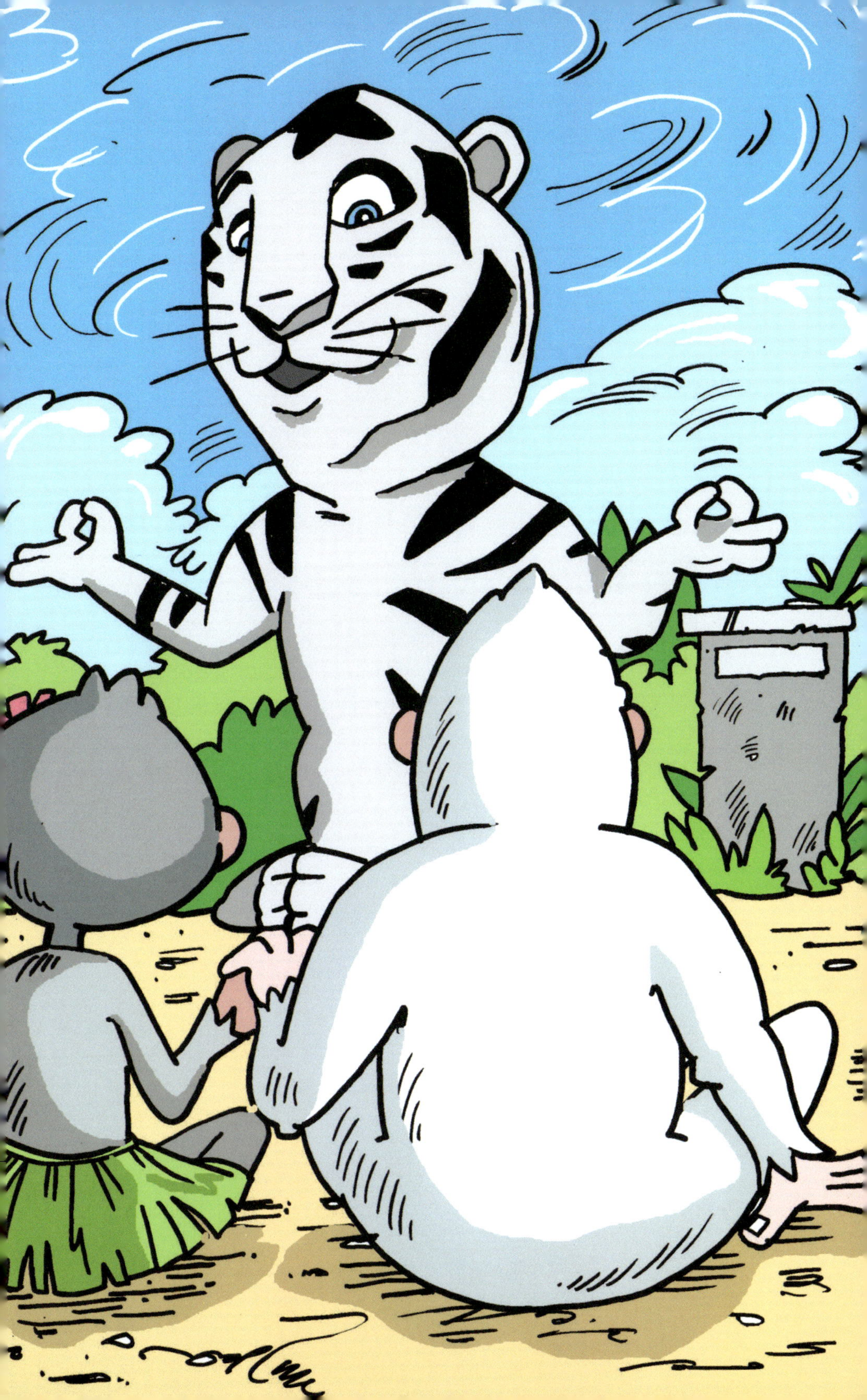

Days later, Snowflake and Hope were back in the Green Bingo Jungle, spreading the great news of the White Tiger. Snowflake had become a hero to all and Hope was his strength and his rock. The adventure had just started … and life always has a next chapter.

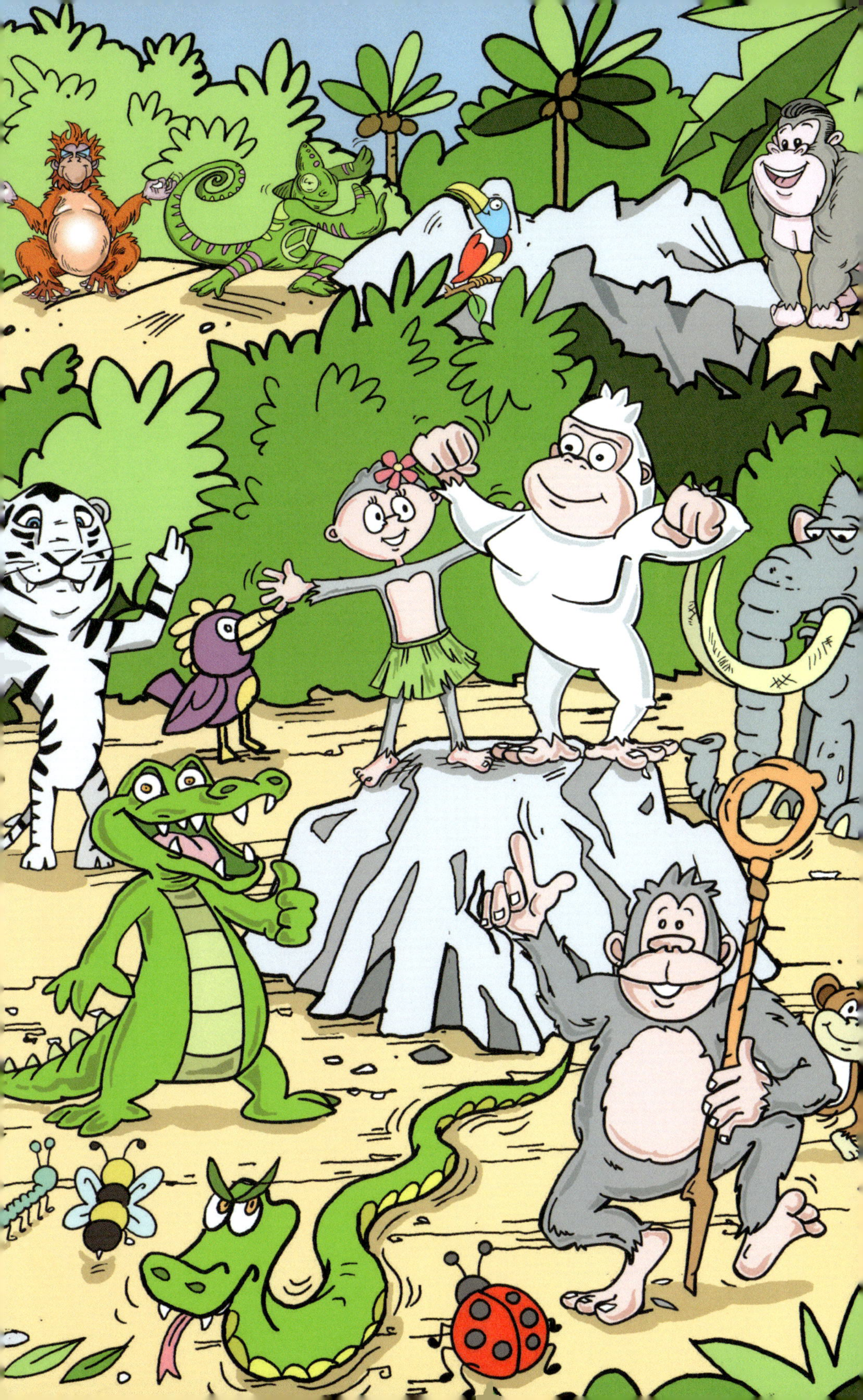

Printed in Great Britain
by Amazon